THE D̶ WORLD

COLLECTORS' EDITION

SF

GOLLANCZ GOLLANCZ

THE BLUE WORLD

Jack Vance

GOLLANCZ

LONDON

Copyright © Jack Vance 1966
All rights reserved

The right of Jack Vance to be identified as the author
of this work has been assserted by him in accordance with
the Copyright, Designs and Patents Act 1988.

The Blue World first appeared as a short story titled
'King Kragen' in *Fantastic Magazine*, copyright © 1964
by Ziff-Davis Publishing Co. Ltd

This edition published in Great Britian in 2003 by
Victor Gollancz
An imprint of The Orion Publishing Group
Orion House, 5 Upper St Martin's Lane, London WC2H 9EA

Distributed in the United States of America
by Sterling Publishing Co., Inc.
387 Park Avenue South, New York, NY 10016-8810

A CIP catalogue record for this book is available
from the British Library

ISBN 0 575 07348 9

Printed and bound in Great Britain by
Clays Ltd, St Ives plc

THE BLUE WORLD

Chapter 1

Among the people of the Floats caste distinctions
were fast losing their old-time importance. The Anarch-
ists and Procurers had disappeared altogether; inter-
caste marriages were by no means uncommon, especially when they involved castes of approximately the
same social status. Society, of course, was not falling
into chaos; the Bezzlers and the Incendiaries still maintained their traditional aloofness; the Advertisermen
still could not evade a subtle but nonetheless general dis-
esteem, and where the castes were associated with a
craft or trade, they functioned with undiminished effec-
tiveness. The Swindlers comprised the vast majority
of those who fished from coracles, and though the once
numerous Peculators had dwindled to a handful, they
still dominated the dye works on Fay Float. Smugglers
boiled varnish, Malpractors pulled teeth. Blackguards
constructed the sponge-arbors in every lagoon; the Hoodwinks completely monopolized the field of hood-winking. This last relationship always excited the curiosity
of the young, who would inquire, "Which first: the Hoodwinks or hood-winking?" To which the elders customarily
replied: "When the Ship of Space discharged the Firsts
upon these blessed floats, there were four Hoodwinks
among the Two Hundred. Later, when the towers were
built and the lamps established, there were hoods to
wink, and it seemed only appropriate that the Hoodwinks should occupy themselves at the trade. It may well
be that matters stood so in the Outer Wildness, before

the Escape. It seems likely. There were undoubtedly lamps to be flashed and hoods to be winked. Of course there is much we do not know, much concerning which the Memoria are either silent or ambiguous."

Whether or not the Hoodwinks had been drawn to the trade by virtue of ancient use, it was now the rare hoodwink who did not in some measure find his vocation upon the towers, either as a rigger, a lamp-tender, or as a full-fledged hoodwink.

Another caste, the Larceners, constructed the towers, which customarily stood sixty to ninety feet high at the center of the float, directly above the primary stalk of the sea-plant. There were usually four legs of woven or laminated withe, which passed through holes in the pad to join a stout stalk twenty or thirty feet below the surface. At the top of the tower was a cupola, with walls of split withe, a roof of varnished and laminated pad-skin. Yardarms extending to either side supported lattices, each carrying nine lamps arranged in a square, together with the hoods and trip-mechanisms. Within the cupola, windows afforded a view across the water to the neighboring floats—a distance as much as the two miles between Green Lamp and Adelvine, or as little as the quarter-mile between Leumar and Populous Equity.

The Master Hoodwink sat at a panel. At his left hand were nine tap-rods, cross-coupled to lamp-hoods on the lattice to his right. Similarly the tap-rods at his right hand controlled the hoods to his left. By this means the configurations he formed and those he received, from his point of view, were of identical aspect and caused him no confusion. During the daytime the lamps were not lit and white targets served the same function. The hoodwink set his configuration with quick strokes of right and left hands, kicked the release, which thereupon flicked the hoods, or shutters, at the respective lamps or targets. Each configuration signified a word; the mastery of a lexicon and a sometimes remarkable dexterity were the Master Hoodwink's stock in trade. All could send at speeds almost that of speech; all knew at least five thousand, and some six, seven, eight, or even nine thousand configurations. The folk of the floats could in varying degrees read the configurations, which were also employed in the keeping of the archives (against the vehement protests of the Scriveners), and in various other communications, public announcements, and messages*.

On Tranque Float, at the extreme east of the group, the Master Hoodwink was one Zander Rohan, a rigorous and exacting old man with a mastery of over seven thousand configurations. His first assistant, Sklar Hast, had well over five thousand configurations at his disposal; precisely how many more he had never publicized. There were two further assistants, as well as three apprentices, two riggers, a lamp-tender, and a maintenance withe-weaver, this latter a Larcener. Zander Rohan tended the tower from dusk until middle evening: the busy hours during which gossip, announcements, news, and notifications regarding King Kragen flickered up and down the fifty-mile line of the floats.

---

*The orthography had been adopted in the earliest days and was highly systematic. The cluster at the left indicated the genus of the idea, the cluster at the right denoted the specific. In such a fashion ⫶ at the left, signified *color*; hence:

White	⫶ ·
Black	⫶ ·
Red	⫶ · ·
Pink	⫶ · ·
Dark Red	· · · ·

and so forth.

Sklar Hast winked hoods during the afternoon; then, when Zander Rohan appeared in the cupola, he looked to maintenance and supervised the apprentices. A relatively young man, Sklar Hast had achieved his status by the simplest and most uncomplicated policy imaginable: With great tenacity he strove for excellence and sought to instill the same standards into the apprentices. He was a positive and direct man, without any great affability, knowing nothing of malice or guile and little of tact or patience. The apprentices resented his brusqueness but respected him; Zander Rohan considered him overpragmatic and deficient in reverence for his betters —which was to say, himself. Sklar Hast cared nothing one way or the other. Zander Rohan must soon retire; in due course Sklar Hast would become Master Hoodwink. He was in no hurry; on this placid, limpid, changeless world, where time drifted rather than throbbed, there was little to be gained by urgency.

Sklar Hast owned a small pad of which he was the sole occupant. The pad, a heart-shaped wad of spongy tissue a hundred feet in diameter, floated at the north of the lagoon. Sklar Hast's hut was of standard construction: withe bent and lashed, then sheathed with sheets of pad-skin, the tough near-transparent membrane peeled from the bottom of the sea-plant pad. All was then coated with well-aged varnish, prepared by boiling sea-plant sap until the water was driven off and the resins amalgamated.

Other vegetation grew in the spongy tissue of the pad: shrubs, a thicket of bamboolike rods yielding good-quality withe, epiphytes hanging from the central spike of the sea-plant. On other pads the plants might be ordered according to aesthetic theory, but Sklar Hast had small taste in these matters, and the center of his pad was little more than an untidy copse of various stalks, fronds, tendrils, and leaves, in various shades of black, green, and rusty orange.

Sklar Hast knew himself for a fortunate man. There was, unfortunately, an obverse to the picture, for those qualities which had won him prestige, position, a private float, were not those calculated to ease him through the careful routines of float society. Only this afternoon he had become involved in a dispute involving a whole complex of basic float principles. Sitting now on the bench before his hut, sipping a cup of wine, Sklar Hast watched lavender dusk settle over the ocean and brooded upon the headstrong folly of Meril Rohan, daughter to Zander Rohan. A breeze ruffled the water, moved the foliage; drawing a deep breath, Sklar Hast felt his anger loosen and drain away. Meril Rohan could do as she pleased; it was folly to exercise himself—either in connection with her or Semm Voiderveg or anything else. Conditions were as they were; if no one else objected, why should he? With this, Sklar Hast smiled a faint, rather bitter, smile, knowing that he could not fully subscribe to this doctrine . . . .

But the evening was far too soft and soothing for contentiousness. In due course events would right themselves, and looking away toward the horizon, Sklar Hast, in a moment of clarity, thought to see the future, as wide and lucid as the dreaming expanse of water and sky. Presently he would espouse one of the girls whom he currently tested—and forever abandon privacy, he reflected wistfully. There was no need for haste. In the case of Meril Rohan . . . But no. She occupied his thoughts merely because of her perverse and headstrong plans in regard to Semm Voiderveg—which did not bear thinking about.

Sklar Hast drained his cup of wine. Folly to worry, folly to fret. Life was good. In the lagoon hung arbors on which grew the succulent spongelike organisms which, when cleaned, plucked and boiled, formed the staple food of the Float folk. The lagoon teemed with edible fish, separated from the predators of the ocean by an enormous net. Much other food was available: spores from the sea-plant fruiting organ, various tendrils and bulbs, as well as the prized flesh of the gray-fish which the swindlers took from the ocean.

Sklar Hast poured himself a second cup of wine and, leaning back, looked up to where the constellations already blazed. Halfway up the southern sky hung a cluster of twenty-five bright stars, from which, so tradition asserted, his ancestors had come, fleeing the persecution of megalomaniac tyrants. Two hundred persons, of various castes, managed to disembark before the Ship of Space foundered in the ocean which spread unbroken around the world. Now, twelve generations later, the two hundred were twenty thousand, scattered along fifty miles of floating sea-plant. The castes, so jealously differentiated during the first few generations, had gradually accommodated themselves to one another and now were even intermingling. There was little to disturb the easy flow of life, nothing harsh or unpleasant—except, perhaps, King Kragen.

Sklar Hast rose, walked to the edge of the float, where only two days before King Kragen had plucked three of his arbors clean. King Kragen's appetite as well as his bulk grew by the year, and Sklar Hast wondered how large King Kragen might eventually become. Was there any limit? During his own lifetime King Kragen had grown perceptibly and now measured perhaps sixty feet in length. Sklar Hast scowled westward across the ocean, in the direction from which King Kragen customarily appeared, moving with long strokes of his four propulsive vanes in a manner to suggest some vast, grotesquely ugly anthropoid swimming the breast-stroke. There, of course, the resemblance to man ended. King Kragen's body was tough black cartilage, a long cylinder riding a heavy rectangle, from the corners of which extended the vanes. The cylinder comprising King Kragen's main bulk opened forward in a maw fringed with four mandibles and eight palps, aft in an anus. Atop this cylinder, somewhat to the front, rose a turret from which the four eyes protruded: two peering forward, two aft. King Kragen was a terrible force for destruction, but luckily could be placated. King Kragen enjoyed copious quantities of sponges, and when his appetite was appeased, he injured no one and did no damage; indeed he kept the area clear of other marauding kragen, which either he killed or sent flapping and skipping in a panic across the ocean.

Sklar Hast returned to the bench, swung sidewise to where he could watch the winks from Tranque Tower. Zander Rohan was at the hoods; Sklar Hast well knew his touch. It was marked by a certain measured crispness, which very gradually was becoming wooden. To the casual eye Zander Rohan's style was clean and deft; his precision and flexibility were those of a Master Hoodwink. But almost insensibly his speed was falling .off, his sense of time was failing; there was a brittle quality to his winking, rather than the supple rhythm of a hoodwink at the height of his powers. Zander Rohan was growing old. Sklar Hast knew that he could outwink Zander Rohan at any time, should he choose to humiliate the old man. This, for all Sklar Hast's bluntness and lack of tact, was the last thing he wished to do. But how long would the old man persist in fulfilling his duties? Even now Zander Rohan had unreasonably delayed his retirement—from jealousy and rancor, Sklar Hast suspected.

The antipathy derived from a whole set of circumstances: Sklar Hast's uncompromising manner, his self-confidence, his professional competence; and then there was the matter of Meril, Zander Rohan's daughter. Five years before, when relations between the two men had been easier, Rohan had extended a number of not too subtle hints that Sklar Hast might well consider Meril as a possible spouse. By every objective standpoint, the prospect should have aroused Sklar Hast's enthusiasm. Meril was of his own caste, the daughter of a guild-master; Sklar Hast's career could not help but be furthered. They were of the same generation, both Elevenths, a matter of no formal importance but which popularly was regarded as desirable and advantageous. And, finally, Meril was by no means uncomely, though somewhat leggy and boyishly abrupt of movement.

What had given Sklar Hast pause was Meril Rohan's unpredictability and perverse behavior. Like most folk of the floats she could read winks, but she also had learned the cursive script of the Firsts. Sklar Hast, with eyes conditioned by the precision and elegance of the hoodwink configurations, considered the script crabbed, sinuous, and cryptic; he was annoyed by its lack of uniformity, even though he recognized and was a connoisseur of the unique and individual style that distinguished each Master Hoodwink. On one occasion he had inquired Meril Rohan's motive for learning the script. "Because I want to read the Memoria," she told him. "Because I wish to become a scrivener."

Sklar Hast had no fault to find with her ambition—he was quite willing that everyone should pursue his own dream—but he was puzzled. "Why go to such effort? The Analects are given in winks. They teach us the substance of the Memoria and eliminate the absurdities."

Meril Rohan laughed in a manner Sklar Hast found somewhat strange. "But it is exactly this that interests me! The absurdities, the contradictions, the allusions— I wonder what they all mean!"

"They mean that the Firsts were a confused and discouraged set of men and women."

"What I want to do," said Meril, "is to make a careful new study of the Memoria. I want to note each of the absurdities and try to understand it, try to relate it to all the other absurdities—because I can't believe that the men who wrote the Memoria considered these passages absurdities."

Sklar Hast gave a shrug of indifference. "Incidentally, your father suggested that you might care to be tested. If you like, you can come to my float any time after tomorrow morning—Coralie Vozelle will then be leaving."

Meril Rohan compressed her lips in mingled amusement and vexation. "My father is trying to marry me off long before I care to be so dealt with. Thank you, I do not care to be tested. Coralie may exert herself on your behalf yet another week, for all of me. Or another month. Or a year."

"As you wish," said Sklar Hast. "It probably would be time wasted, since we obviously have no community of soul."

Shortly thereafter Meril Rohan departed Tranque Float for the Scriveners' Academy on Quatrefoil. Sklar Hast had no idea whether or not Meril had mentioned his solicitation to her father, but thereafter the relationship congealed.

In due course Meril Rohan returned to Tranque with her own copies of the Memoria. The years on Quatrefoil had changed her. She was less careless, less flamboyant, less free with her opinions, and had become almost beautiful, though she still ran to leg and a certain indefinable informality of dress and conduct. Sklar Hast twice had offered to test her. On the first occasion she gave him an absentminded negative; on the second— only a day or two before—she had informed him that Semm Voiderveg was planning to espouse her without benefit of testing.

Sklar Hast found the news incredible, disturbing, unacceptable. Semm Voiderveg, a Hooligan by caste, was Tranque Intercessor, with a prestige second only to that of Ixon Myrex, the Float Arbiter. Nevertheless Sklar Hast found a dozen reasons why Meril Rohan should not become spouse to Semm Voiderveg, and he was not at all diffident in imparting them. "He's an old man! You're hardly more than a girl! He's probably an Eighth! Maybe a Ninth."

"He's not so old. Ten years older than you, or so I should guess. Also he's a Tenth."

"Well, you're an Eleventh, and I'm an Eleventh!"

Meril Rohan looked at him, head at a sidelong tilt, and Sklar Hast suddenly became aware of matters he had never noticed before: the clear luminosity of her skin, the richness of her dark curls, the provocative quality that once had seemed boyish abruptness but now was— something else.

"Bah," muttered Sklar Hast. "You're both insane, the pair of you. He for wiving without a test, you for flinging yourself into the household of a kragen-feeder. You know his caste? He's only a Hooligan."

"What a disrespectful attitude!" she exclaimed. "Semm Voiderveg is Intercessor!"

Sklar Hast peered frowningly at her in an attempt to learn if she was serious. There seemed to be a lightness to her voice, a suppressed levity which he was unable to interpret. "What of it?" he asked. "When you add everything together, the kragen is only a fish. A large fish, true. Still, it seems foolish making so much ceremony over a fish."

"If he were an ordinary fish, your words would have meaning," said Meril Rohan. "King Kragen is not a fish, and he is—extraordinary."

Sklar Hast made a bitter sound. "And you're the one who went to Quatrefoil to become a scrivener! How do you think Voiderveg will take to your unorthodox ideas?"

"I don't know." Meril Rohan gave her head a frivolous toss. "My father wants me married. As spouse to the Intercessor I'll have time to work on my analysis."

"Disgusting," said Sklar Hast, and walked away. Meril Rohan gave her shoulders a shrug and went her own way.

Sklar Hast brooded on the matter during the morning and later in the day approached Zander Rohan: a man as tall as himself, with a great mop of white hair, a neat white beard, a pair of piercing gray eyes, a pinkish complexion, and a manner of constant irascible truculence. In no respect did Meril Rohan resemble her father save in the color of her eyes.

Sklar Hast, who had the least possible facility with tact or subtlety, said, "I've been speaking to Meril. She tells me you want her to espouse Voiderveg."

"Yes," said Zander Rohan. "What of it?"

"It's a poor match. You know Voiderveg: he's portly, pompous, complacent, obstinate, stupid—"

"Here, here!" exclaimed Rohan. "He's Intercessor to Tranque Float! He does my daughter great honor by agreeing to test her!"

"Hmm." Sklar Hast raised his eyebrows. "She told me he'd waived testing."

"As to that, I can't say. If so, the honor is even greater."

Sklar Hast drew a deep breath and made a hard decision. "I'll marry her," he growled. "I'll waive testing. It would be a much better match for her."

Rohan drew back, lips parted in an unpleasant grin. "Why should I give her to an assistant hoodwink when she can have the Intercessor? Especially a man who thinks he's too good for her, to begin with!"

Sklar Hast held back his anger. "I am a Hoodwink, as is she. Do you want her attached to a Hooligan?"

"What difference does it make? He is Intercessor!"

"I'll tell you what difference it makes," said Sklar Hast. "He can't do anything except caper for the benefit of a fish. I am Assistant Master Hoodwink, not just an assistant hoodwink. You know my quality."

Zander Rohan compressed his lips, gave his head a pair of short sharp jerks. "I know your quality—and it's not all it should be. If you expect to master your craft, you had best strike the keys with more accuracy and use fewer paraphrases. When you meet a word you can't wink, let me know and I will instruct you."

Sklar Hast clamped his throat upon the words that struggled to come forth. For all his bluntness, he had no lack of self-control when circumstances warranted, as they did now. Staring eye to eye with Zander Rohan, he weighed the situation. Should he choose, he might require Zander Rohan to defend his rank, and it almost seemed that Rohan were daring him to challenge: for the life of him Sklar Hast could not understand why—except on the basis of sheer personal antipathy. Such contests, once numerous, now were rare, inasmuch as consideration of dignity made resignation of status incumbent upon the loser. Sklar Hast had no real wish to drive Zander Rohan from his position, and he did not care to be driven forth himself . . . . He turned his back and walked away from the Master Hoodwink, ignoring the contemptuous snort that came after him.

At the foot of the tower he stood staring bleakly and unseeingly through the foliage. A few yards away was Zander Rohan's ample three-dome cottage, where, under a pergola draped with sweet-tassel, Meril Rohan sat weaving white cloth at the loom—the spare-time occupation of every female from childhood to old age. Sklar

Hast went to stand by the low fence of woven withe which separated Rohan's plot from the public way. Meril acknowledged his presence with a faint smile and continued with her weaving.

Sklar Hast spoke with measured dignity. "I have been talking with your father. I protested the idea of your espousal to Voiderveg. I told him I would marry you myself." And he turned to look off across the lagoon. "Without testing."

"Indeed. And what did he say?"

"He said no."

Meril, making no comment, continued with her weaving.

"The situation as it stands is ridiculous," said Sklar Hast. "Typical of this outlying and backward float. You would be laughed out of countenance on Apprise or even Sumber."

"If you are unhappy here, why do you not go elsewhere?" asked Meril in a voice of gentle malice.

"I would if I could——I'd leave these insipid floats in their entirety! I'd fly to the far worlds! If I thought they weren't all madhouses."

"Read the Memoria and find out."

"Hmm. After twelve generations all may be changed. The Memoria are a pedant's preserve. Why rake around among the ashes of the past? The scriveners are of no more utility than the intercessors. On second thought, you and Semm Voiderveg will make a good pair. While he invokes blessings upon King Kragen, you can compile a startling new set of Analects."

Meril halted her weaving, frowned down at her hands. "Do you know, I think I will do exactly this?" She rose to her feet, came over to the fence. "Thank you, Sklar Hast!"

Sklar Hast inspected her with suspicion. "Are you serious?"

"Certainly. Have you ever known me otherwise?"

"I've never been sure.... How will a new set of Analects be useful? What's wrong with the old ones?"

"When sixty-one books are condensed into three, a great deal of information is left out."

"Vagueness, ambiguity, introspection: is any of it profitable?"

Meril Rohan pursed her lips. "The inconsistencies are interesting. In spite of the persecutions the Firsts suffered, all express regret at leaving the Home Worlds."

"There must have been other sane folk among the madmen," said Sklar Hast reflectively. "But what of that? Twelve generations are gone; all may be changed. We ourselves have changed, and not for the better. All we care about is comfort and ease. Appease, assuage, compromise. Do you think the Firsts would have capered and danced to an ocean-beast as is the habit of your prospective spouse?"

Meril glanced over Sklar Hast's shoulder; Sklar Hast turned to see Semm Voiderveg the Intercessor, standing by with arms clasped behind his back, head thrust forward: a man of maturity, portly, but by no means ill-favored, with regular features in a somewhat round face. His skin was clear and fresh, his eyes a dark magnetic brown.

"These are impertinent remarks to make of the Intercessor!" said Semm Voiderveg reproachfully. "No matter what you think of him as an individual, the office deserves respect!"

"What office? What do you do?"

"I intercede for the folk of Tranque Float; I secure for us all the benevolence of King Kragen."

Sklar Hast gave an offensive laugh. "I wonder always if you actually believe your own theories."

" 'Theory' is an incorrect word," stated Semm Voiderveg. " 'Science' or 'doxology' is preferable." He went on in a cold voice. "The facts are incontrovertible. King Kragen rules the ocean, he lends us protection; in return we gladly tender him a portion of our bounty. These are the terms of the Covenant."

The discussion was attracting attention among others of the float; already a dozen folk had halted to listen. "In all certainty we have become soft and fearful," said Sklar

Hast. "The Firsts would turn away in disgust. Instead of protecting ourselves, we bribe a beast to do the job."

"Enough!" barked Semm Voiderveg in a sudden cold fury. He turned to Meril, pointed toward the cottage. "Within—that you need not hear the wild talk of this man! An Assistant Master Hoodwink! Astonishing that he has risen so high in the guild!"

With a rather vague smile Meril turned and went into the cottage. Her submission not only irked Sklar Hast; it astounded him.

With a final indignant glance of admonition Semm Voiderveg followed her within.

Sklar Hast turned away toward the lagoon and his own pad. One of the men who had halted called out. "A moment, Sklar Hast! You seriously believe that we could protect our own if King Kragen decided to depart?"

"Certainly," snapped Sklar Hast. "We could at least make the effort! The intercessors want no changes—why should they?"

"You're a troublemaker, Sklar Hast!" called a shrill female voice from the back of the group. "I've known you since you were an infant; you never were less than perverse!"

Sklar Hast pushed through the group, walked through the gathering dusk to the lagoon, ferried himself by coracle to his pad.

He entered the hut, poured himself a cup of wine, and went out to sit on the bench. The halcyon sky and the calm water soothed him, and he was able to summon a grin of amusement for his own vehemence—until he went to look at the arbors plucked bare by King Kragen, whereupon his ill-humor returned.

He watched winks for a few moments, more conscious than ever of Zander Rohan's brittle mannerisms. As he turned away, he noticed a dark swirl in the water at the edge of the net: a black bulk surrounded by glistening cusps and festoons of starlit water. He went to the edge of his float and strained his eyes through the darkness. No question about it: a lesser kragen was probing the net which enclosed Tranque Lagoon!

Chapter 2

Sklar Hast ran across the pad, jumped into his coracle, thrust himself to the central float. He delayed only long enough to tie the coracle to a stake formed of a human femur, then ran at top speed to the hoodwink tower. A mile to the west flickered the Thrasneck lamps, the configurations coming in the unmistakable style of Durdan Farr, the Thrasneck Master Hoodwink: *". . . thirteen . . . bushels . . . of . . . salt . . . lost . . . when . . . a . . . barge . . . took . . . water . . . between . . . Sumber . . . and . . . Adelvine . . ."*

Sklar Hast climbed the ladder, burst into the cupola. Zander Rohan swung about in a surprise that became truculence when he saw Sklar Hast. The pale pink of his face deepened to rose; his lips thrust out; his white hair puffed and glistened as if angry in its own right. It occurred fleetingly to Sklar Hast that Zander Rohan had been in communication with Semm Voiderveg, the subject under discussion doubtless being himself. But now he pointed to the lagoon. "A rogue, breaking the nets. I just saw him. Call King Kragen!"

Zander Rohan instantly forgot his resentment, flashed the cut-in signal. His fingers jammed down rods; he kicked the release. *"Call . . . King . . . Kragen!"* he signaled. *"Rogue . . . in . . . Tranque . . . Lagoon!"*

On Thrasneck Float Durdan Farr relayed the message to the tower on Bickle Float, and so along the line of floats to Sciona at the far west, which thereupon returned the signal: *"King . . . Kragen . . . is . . . nowhere*

21

...at...hand." Back down the line of towers flickered the message, returning to Tranque Float in something short of twelve minutes.

Sklar Hast had not awaited the return message. Descending the ladder, he ran back to the lagoon. The kragen had cut open a section of the net and now hung in the gap, plucking sponges from a nearby arbor. Sklar Hast pushed through the crowd which stood watching in awe. "Ha! Ho!" cried Sklar Hast, flapping his arms. "Leave us, you dismal black beast!"

The kragen ignored him and with insulting assurance continued to pluck sponges and convey them to its maw. Sklar Hast picked up a heavy knurled joint from a sea-plant stem, hurled it at the turret, striking the forward eye-tube. The kragen recoiled, worked its vanes angrily. The folk on the float muttered uneasily, though a few laughed in great gratification. "There's the way to deal with kragen!" exulted Irvin Belrod, a wizened old Advertiserman. "Strike another blow!"

Sklar Hast picked up a second joint, but someone grabbed his arm—Semm Voiderveg, who spoke in a sharp voice. "What ill-conceived acts are you committing?"

Sklar Hast jerked free. "Watch and you'll see." He turned toward the kragen, but Voiderveg stepped in his way. "This is arrogance! Have you forgotten the Covenant? King Kragen has been notified; let him deal with the nuisance. This is his prerogative!"

"While the beast destroys our net? Look!" Sklar Hast pointed across the water to Thrasneck Tower, where the return message now flickered: *"King ... Kragen ... is nowhere ... to ... be ... seen."*

Semm Voiderveg gave a stiff nod. "I will issue a notice to all intercessors and King Kragen will be summoned."

"Summoned how? By calling into the night with lamps held aloft?"

"Concern yourself with hoodwinking," said Semm Voiderveg in the coldest of voices. "The intercessors will deal with King Kragen."

Sklar Hast turned, hurled the second joint, which struck the beast in the maw. It emitted a hiss of annoyance, thrashed with vanes, and breaking wide the net, surged into the lagoon. Here it floated, rumbling and hissing, a beast perhaps fifteen feet in length.

"Observe what you have accomplished!" cried Semm Voiderveg in a ringing voice. "Are you satisfied? The net is now broken and no mistake."

All turned to watch the kragen, which swung its vanes and surged through the water, a caricature of a man performing the breast-stroke. Starlight danced and darted along the disturbed water, outlining the gliding black bulk. Sklar Hast cried out in fury: the brute was headed for his arbors, so recently devastated by the appetite of King Kragen! He ran to his coracle, thrust himself to his pad. Already the kragen had extended its palps and was feeling for sponges. Sklar Hast sought for an implement which might serve as a weapon; there was nothing to hand: a few articles fashioned from human bones and fish cartilage, a wooden bucket, a mat of woven fiber.

Leaning against the hut was a boat-hook, a stalk ten feet long, carefully straightened, scraped, and seasoned, to which a hook-shaped human rib had been lashed. He took it up and now from the central pad came Semm Voiderveg's cry of remonstrance. "Sklar Hast! What do you do?"

Sklar Hast paid no heed. He ran to the edge of the pad, jabbed the boat-hook at the kragen's turret. It scraped futilely along the resilient cartilage. The kragen swung up a palp, knocked the pole aside. Sklar Hast jabbed the pole with all his strength at what he considered the kragen's most vulnerable area: a soft pad of receptor-endings directly above the maw. Behind, he heard Semm Voiderveg's outraged protest: "This is not to be done! Desist! Desist!"

The kragen quivered at the blow, twisted its massive turret to gaze at Sklar Hast. It swung up its fore-vane, slashing at Sklar Hast, who leaped back with inches to spare. From the central pad Semm Voiderveg bawled, "By no means molest the kragen; it is a matter for the King! We must respect the King's authority!"

Sklar Hast stood back in fury as the kragen resumed its

feeding. As if to punish Sklar Hast for his assault, it passed close beside the arbors, worked its vanes, and the arbors—sea-plant stalk lashed with fiber—collapsed. Sklar Hast groaned. "No more than you deserve," called out Semm Voiderveg with odious complacence. "You interfered with the duties of King Kragen—now your arbors are destroyed. This is justice."

"Justice? Bah!" bellowed Sklar Hast. "Where is King Kragen? We feed the gluttonous beast; why isn't he at hand when we need him?"

"Come, come," admonished Semm Voiderveg. "This is hardly the tone in which to speak of King Kragen!"

Sklar Hast groped through the shadows, retrieved the boat-hook, to find that the bone had broken, leaving a sharp point. With all his power, Sklar Hast thrust this at the kragen's eye. The point slid off the hemispherical lens, plunged into the surrounding tissue. The kragen humped almost double, thrust itself clear of the water, fell with a great splash and, sounding, sank from sight. Waves crossed the lagoon, reflected from the surrounding floats, subsided. The lagoon was quiet.

Sklar Hast went to his coracle, pushed himself to the mainland, joined the group which stood peering down into the water.

"Is it dead?" inquired one Morgan Resly, a Swindler of good reputation.

"No such luck," growled Sklar Hast. "Next time—"

"Next time—what?" demanded Semm Voiderveg.

"Next time, I'll kill it."

"And what of King Kragen, who reserves such affairs to himself?"

"King Kragen doesn't care a fig one way or the other," said Sklar Hast. "Except for one matter: if we took to the habit of killing kragen, we might begin to look him over with something of the sort in mind."

Semm Voiderveg made a guttural sound, threw up his hands, turned, walked rapidly away.

Poe Belrod, nominal Elder of the Belrod clan even though Irvin surpassed him in actual age, asked Sklar Hast, "Can you really kill a kragen?"

"I don't know," said Sklar Hast. "I haven't given the notion any thought—so far."

"They're a tough beast." Poe Belrod shook his big, crafty head in doubt. "And then we'd have the wrath of King Kragen to fear."

"It's a matter to think about," said Sklar Hast.

Timmons Valby, an Extorter, spoke. "How is King Kragen to know? He can't be everywhere at once."

"He knows, he knows all!" stated a nervous old Incendiary. "All goes well along the floats; we must not cause grief and woe from pride; remember Kilborn's Dictum from the Analects: 'Pride goeth before a fall!'"

"Yes, indeed, but recall Baxter's Dictum: 'There shall no evil happen to the just, but the wicked shall be filled with mischief!'"

The group stood silent a moment, looking over the lagoon, but the kragen did not reappear.

"He's broken through the bottom and departed," said Morgan Resly, the Swindler.

The group gradually dispersed, some going to their huts, others to Tranque Inn—a long structure furnished with tables, benches, and a counter where wines, syrups, spice-cake, and pepperfish were to be had. Sklar Hast joined this latter group, but sat morosely to the side while every aspect of the evening's events was discussed. Everyone was vehement in his detestation of the rogue kragen but some quetioned the method used by Sklar Hast. Jonas Serbano, a Bezzler, felt that Sklar Hast had acted somewhat too precipitously. "In matters of this sort, where King Kragen is concerned, all must consult. The wisdom of many is preferable to the headlong rashness of one, no matter how great the provocation."

Eyes went to Sklar Hast, but he made no response, and it remained for one of the younger Belrods to remark, "That's all very well, but by the time everyone argues and debates, the sponges are eaten and gone."

"Better lose an arbor of sponges than risk the displeasure of King Kragen!" replied Jonas Serbano tartly. "The sea and all that transpires therein is his realm; we trespass at our peril!"

Young Garth Gasselton, an Extorter by caste though a pad-stripper by trade, spoke with the idealistic fervor of youth. "If conditions were as they should be, we would be masters of all: float, lagoon, and sea alike! The sponges would then be our own; we would need bow our heads to no one!"

At a table across the room sat Ixon Myrex, the Tranque Arbiter, a Bezzler of great physical presence and moral conviction. To this moment he had taken no part in the conversation, sitting with his massive head averted, thus signifying a desire for privacy. Now he slowly turned and fixed a somewhat baleful stare upon young Garth Gasselton. "You speak without reflection. Are we then so omnipotent that we can simply wave our hands across the sea and command all to our sway? You must recognize that comfort and plenty are neither natural endowments nor our rightful due, but benefits of the most tentative nature imaginable. In short, we exist by the indulgence of King Kragen, and never must we lose sight of the fact!"

Young Gasselton blinked down at his cup of syrup, but old Irvin Belrod was not so easily abashed. "I'll tell you one thing that you're forgetting, Arbiter Myrex. King Kragen is as he is because we made him so. At the beginning he was a normal kragen, maybe a bit bigger and smarter than the others. He's what he is today because somebody made the mistake of truckling to him. Now the mistake has been made, and I'll grant you that King Kragen is wise and clever and occasionally serves us by scaring away the rogues—but where will it end?"

Wall Bunce, an old Larcener crippled by a fall from the Tranque tower yardarms, held up an emphatic finger. "Never forget Cardinal's Dictum from the Analects: 'Whoever is willing to give will never lack someone to take.' "

Into the inn came Semm Voiderveg and Zander Rohan. They seated themselves beside Ixon Myrex: the three most influential men of the float. After giving Voiderveg and Rohan greeting, Ixon Myrex returned to

Wall Bunce. "Don't go quoting the Analects to me, because I can quote in return: 'The most flagrant fool is the man who doesn't know when he's well off!' "

"I give you, 'If you start a fight with your hands in your pockets, you'll have warm hands but a bloody nose!' " called Wall Bunce.

Ixon Myrex thrust out his chin. "I don't intend to quote Dicta at you all evening, Wall Bunce."

"It's a poor way to win an argument," Irvin Belrod remarked.

"I am by no manner of means conducting an argument," stated Ixon Myrex ponderously. "The subject is too basic; it affects the welfare of Tranque and of all the floats. There certainly cannot be two sides to a matter as fundamental as this!"

"Here, now," protested a young scrivener. "You beg the question! All of us favor continued prosperity and welfare. We're at odds because we define 'welfare' differently."

Ixon Myrex looked down the bridge of his nose. "The welfare of Tranque Float is not so abstruse a matter," he said. "We require merely an amplitude of food and a respect for institutions established by wise men of the past."

Semm Voiderveg, looking off into mid-air, spoke in measured minatory voice. "Tonight an exceedingly rash act was performed, by a man who should know better. I simply cannot understand a mentality which so arrogantly preempts to itself a decision concerning the welfare of the whole float."

Sklar Hast at last was stung. He gave a sarcastic chuckle. "I understand your mentality well enough. If it weren't for King Kragen, you'd have to work like everyone else. You've achieved a sinecure, and you don't want a detail changed, no matter how much hardship and degradation are involved."

"Hardship? There is plenty for all! And degradation? Do you dare use the word in connection with myself or Arbiter Myrex or Master Hoodwink Rohan? I assure you that these men are by no means degraded, and I believe that they resent the imputation as keenly as I do myself!"

Sklar Hast grinned. "There's a dictum to cover all that: 'If the shoe fits, wear it.'"

Zander Rohan burst out, "This caps all! Sklar Hast, you disgrace your caste and your calling! I have no means of altering the circumstances of your birth, but thankfully, I am Guild-Master. I assure you that your career as a hoodwink is at an end!"

"Bah," sneered Sklar Hast. "On what grounds?"

"Turpitude of the character!" roared Zander Rohan. "This is a passage of the bylaws, as well you know!"

Sklar Hast gave Zander Rohan a long, slow inspection, as before. He sighed and made his decision. "There's also a passage to the effect that a man shall be Guild-Master only so long as he maintains a paramount proficiency. I challenge not only your right to pass judgment but your rank as Guild-Master as well."

Silence held the inn. Zander Rohan spoke in a choked voice. "You think you can outwink me?"

"At any hour of the day or night."

"Why have you not made this vaunted ability manifest before?"

"If you want to know the truth, I did not wish to humiliate you."

Zander Rohan slammed his fist upon the table. "Very well. We shall see who is to be humiliated. Come: to the tower!"

Sklar Hast raised his eyebrows in surprise. "You are in haste?"

"You said, 'Any hour of the day or night.'"

"As you wish. Who will judge?"

"Arbiter Myrex, of course. Who else?"

"Arbiter Myrex will serve well enough, provided we have others to keep time and note errors."

"I appoint Semm Voiderveg; he reads with great facility."

Sklar Hast pointed to others in the room, persons he knew to be keen of eye and deft at reading winks. "Rubal

Gallager—Freeheart Noe—Herlinger Showalter. I appoint these to read winks and note errors."

Zander Rohan made no objection; all in the inn arose and crossed to the tower.

The space under the tower was enclosed by a wall of withe and varnished pad-skin. On the first level was a shed given over to practice mechanisms; on the second were stores: spare hoods, oil for the lamps, connection cords, and records; the third and fourth levels housed apprentices, assistant hoodwinks on duty, and maintenance larceners.

Into the first level trooped Zander Rohan and Sklar Hast, followed by those whom they had appointed judges, and ten or twelve others—as many as the shed could contain. Lamps were turned up, benches pushed back, window shutters raised for ventilation.

Zander Rohan went to the newest of the two practice machines, ran his fingers over the keys, kicked the release. He frowned, thrust out his lip, went to the older of the machines, which was looser and easier but with considerably more backlash. The tighter machine required more effort but allowed more speed. He signaled to the apprentices, who stood looking down from the second level. "Oil. Lubricate the connections. Is this how you maintain the equipment?"

The apprentices hastened to obey.

Sklar Hast ran his fingers over the keys of both machines and decided to use the newer, if the choice was his. Zander Rohan went to the end of the room where he conferred in quiet tones with Ixon Myrex and Semm Voiderveg. All three turned, glanced at Sklar Hast, who stood waiting impassively. Antagonism hung heavy in the room.

Ixon Myrex and Semm Voiderveg came toward Sklar Hast. "Do you have any conditions or exceptions to make?" ·

"Tell me what you propose," said Sklar Hast. "Then I'll tell you my conditions or exceptions."

"We propose nothing unusual—in fact, a test similar to those at the Aumerge Tournament during the Year of Waldemar's Drive."

Sklar Hast gave a curt nod. "Four selections from the Analects?"

"Precisely."

"What selections?"

"Apprentice exercises might be most convenient, but I don't think Master Rohan is particular in this case."

"Nor I. Apprentice exercises will be well enough."

"I propose we use tournament weighing: The best score is mutiplied by fifty, the next by thirty, the next by twenty, the worst by ten. This ensures that your best effort will receive the greatest weight."

Sklar Hast reflected. The system of weighting tended to favor the efforts of the nervous or erratic operator, while the steadier and more consistent operator was handicapped. Still, under the present circumstances, it made small difference: neither he nor Zander Rohan were typically given to effulgent bursts of speed. "I agree. What of miswinks?"

"Each error or miswink to add three seconds to the score."

Sklar Hast acquiesced. There was further discussion of a technical nature, as to what constituted an error, how the errors should be noted and reckoned in regard to the operation of the clock.

Finally all possible contingencies had been discussed. The texts were selected: Exercises 61, 62, 63, 64, all excerpts from the Analects, which in turn had been derived from the sixty-one volumes of Memoria.

Before assenting to the exercises, Zander Rohan donned the spectacles which he recently had taken to using—two lenses of clear gum, melted, cast and held in frames of laminated withe—and carefully read the exercises. Sklar Hast followed suit, though through his work with the apprentices he was intimately acquainted with them. The contestants might use either machine, and both elected to use the new machine. Each man would wink an exercise in turn, and Zander Rohan signified that he wished Sklar Hast to wink first.

Sklar Hast went to the machine, arranged Exercise 61 in front of him, stretched his brown fingers, tested the action of keys and kick-rods. Across the room sat the judges, while Arbiter Myrex controlled the clock. At this moment the door slid back, and into the shed came Meril Rohan.

Zander Rohan made a peremptory motion, which she ignored. Intercessor Voiderveg frowned and held up an admonitory finger, which she heeded even less. Sklar Hast looked once in her direction, meeting her bright gaze, and could not decide on its emotional content: Scorn? Detestation? Amusement? It made no great difference.

"Ready!" called Ixon Myrex. Sklar Hast bent slightly forward, strong hands and tense fingers poised. "Set! Wink!"

Sklar Hast's hands struck down at the keys; his foot kicked the release. The first configuration, the second, the third. Sklar Hast winked deliberately, gradually loosening, letting his natural muscular rhythm augment his speed.

—even were we able to communicate with the Home Worlds, I wonder if we would now choose to do so. Ignoring the inevitable prosecution which would ensue (owing to our unique background)—as I say, not even considering this—we have gained here something which none of us have ever known before: a sense of achievement on a level other than what I will call 'social manipulation.' We are, by and large, happy on the floats. There is naturally much homesickness, nostalgia, vain regrets—how could this be avoided? Would they be less poignant on New Ossining? This is a question all of us have argued at length, to no decision. The facts are that we all seem to be facing the realities of our new life with a fortitude and equanimity of which we probably did not suspect ourselves capable.

"End!" called Sklar Hast. Ixon Myrex checked the clock. "One hundred forty-six seconds."

Sklar Hast moved back from the machine. A good

time, though not dazzling, and by no means his best speed. "Mistakes?" he inquired.

"No mistakes," stated Rubal Gallager.

Norm time was one hundred fifty-two seconds, which gave him a percentum part score of 6/162, or 3.95 minus.

Zander Rohan poised himself before the machine and at the signal winked forth the message in his usual somewhat brittle style. Sklar Hast listened carefully, and it seemed as if the Master Hoodwink were winking somewhat more deliberately than usual.

Zander Rohan's time was one hundred forty-five seconds; he made no mistakes, and his score was 4.21 minus. He stepped to the side with the trace of a smile. Sklar Hast glanced from the corner of his eye to Meril Rohan, for no other reason than idle curiosity—or so he told himself. Her face revealed nothing.

He set Exercise 62 before him. Ixon Myrex gave the signal; Sklar Hast's hands struck out the first wink. Now he was easy and loose, and his fingers worked like pistons.

Exercise 62, like 61, was an excerpt from the Memorium of Eleanor Morse:

A hundred times we have discussed what to my mind is perhaps the most astonishing aspect of our new community on the float: the sense of trust, of interaction, of mutual responsibility. Who could have imagined from a group of such diverse backgrounds, with such initial handicaps (whether innate or acquired I will not presume to speculate), there might arise so placid, so ordered, and so cheerful a society. Our elected leader, like myself, is an embezzler. Some of our most tireless and self-sacrificing workers were previously peculators, hooligans, goons: One could never match the individuals with their past lives. The situation, of course, is not unanimous, but to an amazing extent old habits and attitudes have been superseded by a positive sense of participation in the life of something larger than self. To most of us it is

*as if we had regained a lost youth or, indeed, a youth
we never had known.*

"End!" called Sklar Hast.

Ixon Myrex stopped the clock. "Time: one hundred
eighty-two seconds. Norm: two hundred seconds. Mistakes? None."

Sklar Hast's score was a solid 9 minus. Zander Rohan winked a blazing-fast but nervous and staccato one-hundred seventy-nine seconds, but made at least two mistakes. Rubal Gallager and Herlinger Showalter claimed to have detected enough of a waver in one of the corner hoods to qualify as a third error, but Freeheart Noe had not noticed, and both Semm Voiderveg and Ixon Myrex insisted that the configuration had been clearly winked. Nevertheless, with a penalty of six seconds, his time became a hundred eighty-five with a score of 15/200 or 7.50 per cent minus.

Sklar Hast approached the third exercise thoughtfully. If he could make a high score on this third exercise, Zander Rohan, already tense, might well press and blow the exercise completely.

He poised himself. "Wink!" cried Ixon Myrex. And again Sklar Hast's fingers struck the tabs. The exercise was from the Memorium of Wilson Snyder, a man of unstated caste:

Almost two years have elapsed, and there is no question but what we are an ingenious group. Alertness, ingenuity, skill at improvisation: These are our characteristics. Or, as our detractors would put it, a low simian cunning. Well, so be it. Another trait luckily common to all of us (more or less) is a well-developed sense of resignation, or perhaps fatalism is the word, toward circumstances beyond our control. Hence we are a far happier group than might be a corresponding number of, say, musicians or scientists or even law-enforcement officers. Not that these professions go unrepresented among our little band. Jora Alvan—an accomplished flautist. James Brunet—

professor of physical science at Southwestern University. Howard Gallagher—a high-ranking police official. And myself—but no! I adhere to my resolution, and I'll say nothing of my past life. Modesty? I wish I could claim as much!

"End!" Sklar Hast drew a deep breath and stepped back from the machine. He did not look toward Zander Rohan; it would have been an act of malignant gloating to have done so. For he had driven the machine as fast as its mechanism permitted. No man alive could have winked faster, with a more powerful driving rhythm.

Ixon Myrex examined the clock. "Time: one hundred seventy-two seconds," he said reluctantly. "Norm... This seems incorrect. Two hundred eight?"

"Two hundred eight is correct," said Rubal Gallager dryly. "There were no mistakes."

Ixon Myrex and Semm Voiderveg chewed their lips glumly. Freeheart Noe calculated the score: 36/208, or a remarkable 17.3 minus!

Zander Rohan stepped forward bravely enough and poised himself before the machine. "Wink!" cried Ixon Myrex in a voice that cracked from tension. And Zander Rohan's once precise fingers stiffened with his own fear and tension, and his careful rhythm faltered. All in the room stood stiff and embarrassed.

Finally he called: "End!"

Ixon Myrex read the clock. "Two hundred and one seconds."

"There were two mistakes," said Semm Voiderveg. Rubal Gallager started to speak, then held his tongue. He had noted at least five instances which an exacting observer—such as Zander Rohan himself—might have characterized as error. But the contest was clearly one-sided. Two hundred and one seconds, plus six penalty seconds gave Zander Rohan a score of 1/208 or .48 minus.

The fourth exercise was from the Memorium of Hedwig Swin, who, like Wilson Snyder, maintained reserve in regard to her caste.

Ixon Myrex set the clock with unwilling fingers, called out the starting signal. Sklar Hast winked easily, without effort, and the configurations spilled forth in a swift certain flow:

A soft, beautiful world! A world of matchless climate, indescribable beauty, a world of water and sky, with, to the best of my knowledge, not one square inch of solid ground. Along the equator where the seaplants grow, the ocean must be comparatively shallow, though no one has plumbed the bottom. Quite certainly this world will never be scarred and soiled by an industrial civilization, which, of course, is all very well. Still, speaking for myself, I would have welcomed a jut of land or two: a good honest mountain, with rocks and trees with roots gripping the soil, a stretch of beach, a few meadows, fields, and orchards. But beggars can't be choosers, and compared with our original destination this world is heaven.

"End!"

Ixon Myrex spoke tersely. "Time: one hundred forty-one. Norm: one hundred sixty."

All was lost for Zander Rohan. To win he would have to wink for a score of twenty-five or thirty, or perhaps even higher. He knew he could not achieve this score and winked without hope and without tension and achieved his highest score of the test: a strong 12.05 minus. Nonetheless he had lost, and now, by the guild custom, he must resign his post and give way to Sklar Hast.

He could not bring himself to speak the words. Meril turned on her heel, departed the building.

Zander Rohan finally turned to Sklar Hast. He had started to croak a formal admission of defeat when Semm Voiderveg stepped quickly forward, took Zander Rohan's arm, pulled him aside.

He spoke in urgent tones while Sklar Hast looked on with a sardonic grin. Ixon Myrex joined the conversation and pulled his chin doubtfully. Zander Rohan stood less erect than usual, his fine bush of white hair limp and his beard twisted askew. From time to time he shook his head in forlorn but unemphatic objection to Semm Voiderveg's urgings.

But Semm Voiderveg had his way and turned toward Sklar Hast. "A serious defect in the test has come to light. I fear it cannot be validated."

"Indeed?" asked Sklar Hast. "And how is this?"

"It appears that you work daily with these exercises, during your instruction of the apprentices. In short, you have practiced these exercises intensively, and the contest thereby is not a fair one."

"You selected the exercises yourself."

"Possibly true. It was nevertheless your duty to inform us of your familiarity with the matter."

"In sheer point of fact," said Sklar Hast, "I am not familiar with the exercises and had not winked them since I was an apprentice myself."

Semm Voiderveg shook his head. "I find this impossible to believe. I, for one, refuse to validate the results of this so-called contest, and I believe that Arbiter Myrex feels much the same disgust and indignation as I do myself."

Zander Rohan had the grace to croak a protest. "Let the results stand. I cannot explain away the score."

"By no means!" exclaimed Semm Voiderveg. "A Master Hoodwink must be a man of utter probity. Do we wish in this august position one who—"

Sklar Hast said in a gentle voice, "Be careful of your words, Intercessor. The penalties for slander are strict, as Arbiter Myrex can inform you."

"Slander exists if truth is absent or malice is the motivation. I am concerned only for the well-being of Tranque Float, and the conservation of traditional morality. Is it slander, then, if I denounce you as a near-approach to a common cheat?"

Sklar Hast took a slow step forward, but Rubal Gallager took his arm. Sklar Hast turned to Arbiter Myrex. "And what do you say to all this, you who are Arbiter?"

Ixon Myrex's forehead was damp. "Perhaps we should have used other texts for the test. Even though you had no hand in the selection."

To the side stood two or three members of the Belrod clan, deep-divers for stalk and withe, of the Advertiser-man caste, generally prone to a rude and surly vulgarity. Now Poe Belrod, the Caste Elder, a squat, large-featured man, slapped his hand to his thigh in indignation. "Surely, Arbiter Myrex, you cannot subscribe to a position so obviously arbitrary and contrived? Remember, you are elected to decide issues on the basis of justice and not orthodoxy!"

Ixon Myrex flew into a rage. "Do you question my integrity? An abuse was brought to my attention by the Intercessor; it seems a real if unfortunate objection, and I declare the test invalid. Zander Rohan remains Master Hoodwink."

Sklar Hast started to speak, but now there was a cry from outside the shed: "The kragen has returned! The kragen swims in the lagoon!"

Chapter 3

Sklar Hast pushed outside, went at a run to the lagoon, followed by all those who had witnessed the test.

Floating in the center of the lagoon was the black hulk of the kragen, vanes restlessly swirling the water. For a moment the forward-looking eyes surveyed the crowd on the main float; then it surged slowly forward, mandibles clicking with a significant emphasis. Whether or not it recognized Sklar Hast was uncertain; nevertheless it swam toward where he stood, then suddenly gave a great thrust of the vanes, plunged full speed ahead to throw a wave up over the edge of the pad. As it struck the edge, it flung out a vane, and the flat end splashed past Sklar Hast's chest. He staggered back in surprise and shock, to trip on a shrub and fall.

From nearby came Semm Voiderveg's chuckle. "Is this the kragen you spoke so confidently of killing?"

Sklar Hast regained his feet and stood looking silently at the kragen. Starlight glinted from the oily black back as if it were covered with satin. It swung to the side and began plucking with great energy at a set of convenient sponge arbors, which, as luck would have it, were the property of the Belrods, and Poe Belrod called out a series of bitter curses.

Sklar Hast looked about him. At least a hundred folk of Tranque Float stood nearby. Sklar Hast pointed. "The vile beast of the sea plunders us. I say we should kill it, and all other kragen who seek to devour our sponges!" Semm Voiderveg emitted a high-pitched croak. "Are you insane? Someone, pour water on this maniac hoodwink, who has too long focused his eyes on flashing lights!"

In the lagoon the kragen tore voraciously at the choicest Belrod sponges, and the Belrods emitted a series of anguished hoots.

"I say, kill the beast!" cried Sklar Hast. "The king despoils us; must we likewise feed all the kragen of the ocean?"

"Kill the beast!" echoed the younger Belrods.

Semm Voiderveg gesticulated in vast excitement, but Poe Belrod shoved him roughly aside. "Quiet, let us listen to the hoodwink. How could we kill the kragen? Is it possible?"

"No!" cried Semm Voiderveg. "Of course it is not possible! Nor is it wise or proper! What of our covenant with King Kragen?"

"King Kragen be damned!" cried Poe Belrod roughly. "Let us hear the hoodwink. Come then: do you have any method in mind by which the kragen can be destroyed?"

Sklar Hast looked dubiously through the dark toward the great black hulk. "I think—yes. A method that requires the strength of many men."

Poe Belrod waved his hand toward those who had come to watch the kragen. "Here they stand."

"Come," said Sklar Hast. He walked back toward the center of the float. Thirty or forty men followed him, mostly Swindlers, Advertisermen, Blackguards, Extorters and Larceners. The remainder hung dubiously back.

Sklar Hast led the way to a pile of poles stacked for the construction of a new storehouse. Each pole, fabricated from withes laid lengthwise and bound in glue, was twenty feet long by eight inches in diameter and combined great strength with lightness. Sklar Hast selected a pole even thicker—the ridge beam. "Pull this pole forth, lay it on a trestle!"

While this was being accomplished, he looked about and signaled Rudolf Snyder, a Ninth, though a man no older than himself of the long-lived Incendiary Caste, which now monopolized the preparation of fiber, the lay-ing of rope and plaits. "I need two hundred feet of hawser, stout enough to lift the kragen. If there is none of this, then we must double or redouble smaller rope to the same effect."

Rudolf Snyder took four men to help him and brought rope from the warehouse.

Sklar Hast worked with great energy, rigging the pole in accordance with his plans. "Now lift! Carry all to the edge of the pad!"

Excited by his urgency, the men shouldered the pole, carried it close to the lagoon, and at Sklar Hast's direction set it down with one end resting on the hard fiber of a rib. The other end, to which two lengths of hawser were tied, rested on a trestle and almost overhung the water. "Now," said Sklar Hast, "now we kill the kragen." He made a noose at the end of a hawser, advanced toward the kragen, which watched him through the rear-pointing eyes of its turret. Sklar Hast moved slowly, so as not to alarm the creature, which continued to pluck sponges with a contemptuous disregard.

Sklar Hast approached the edge of the pad. "Come, beast," he called. "Ocean brute! Come closer. Come." He bent, splashed water at the kragen. Provoked, it surged toward him. Sklar Hast waited, and just before it swung its vane, he tossed the noose over its turret. He signaled his men. "Now!" They heaved on the line, dragged the thrashing kragen through the water. Sklar Hast guided the line to the end of the pole. The kragen surged suddenly forward; in the confusion and the dark the men heaving on the rope fell backward. Sklar Hast seized the slack and, dodging a murderous slash of the kragen's fore-vane, flung a hitch around the end of the pole. He danced back. "Now!" he called. "Pull, pull! Both lines! The beast is as good as dead!"

On each of the pair of hawsers tied to the head of the pole twenty men heaved. The pole raised on its base; the line tautened around the kragen's turret; the men dug in their heels; the base of the pole bit into the hard rib. The pole raised farther, braced by the angle of the ropes. With majestic deliberation the thrashing kragen was lifted from the water and swung up into the air. From the others who watched passively came a murmurous moan of fascination. Semm Voiderveg, who had been standing somewhat apart, made a gesture of horror and walked swiftly away.

Ixon Myrex, the Arbiter, for reasons best known to himself, was nowhere to be seen, nor was Zander Rohan.

The kragen made gulping noises, reached its vanes this way and that, to no avail. Sklar Hast surveyed the creature, somewhat at a loss as to how next to proceed. His helpers were looking at the kragen in awe, uncomfortable at their own daring. Already they stole furtive glances out over the ocean, which, perfectly calm, glistened with the reflections of the blazing constellations. Sklar Hast thought to divert their attention. "The nets!" he called out to those who watched. "Where are the hooligans? Repair the nets before we lose all our fish! Are you helpless?"

Certain net-makers, a trade dominated by the Hooligans, detached themselves from the group and went out to repair the broken net.

Sklar Hast returned to a consideration of the dangling kragen. At his orders the hawsers supporting the tilted pole were made fast to ribs on the surface of the pad; the men now gathered gingerly about the dangling kragen and speculated as to the best means to kill the creature. Perhaps it was already dead. To test this theory, a lad of the Belrods prodded the kragen with a length of stalk and suffered a broken collarbone from a quick blow of the fore-vane.

Sklar Hast stood somewhat apart, studying the creature. Its hide was tough; its cartilaginous tissue even tougher. He sent one man for a boat-hook, another for a sharp femur-stake, and from the two fashioned a spear.

The kragen hung limp, the vanes swaying, occasionally twitching. Sklar Hast moved forward cautiously, touched the point of the spear to the side of the turret, thrust with all his weight. The point entered the tough hide perhaps half an inch, then broke. The kragen jerked, snorted, a vane slashed out. Sklar Hast sensed the dark

flicker of motion, dodged, and felt the air move beside
his face. The spear shaft hurtled out over the pond; the
vane struck the pole on which the kragen hung, bruising
the fibers.

"What a quarrelsome beast!" muttered Sklar Hast.
"Bring more rope; we must prevent such demonstra-
tions."

From the side came a harsh command: "You are
madmen; why do you risk the displeasure of King Kragen? I decree that you desist from your rash acts!"

This was the voice of Ixon Myrex, who now had appeared on the scene. Sklar Hast could not ignore Ixon
Myrex as he had Semm Voiderveg. He considered the
dangling kragen, looked about at the faces of his comrades. Some were hesitating; Ixon Myrex was not a
man to be trifled with.

Sklar Hast spoke in a voice which he felt to be calm
and reasonable. "The kragen is destroying our arbors.
If the King is slothful about his duties, why should we
permit—"

Ixon Myrex's voice shook with wrath. "That is no
way to speak! You violate the Covenant!"

Sklar Hast spoke even more politely than before. "King
Kragen is nowhere to be seen. The intercessors who claim
such large power run back and forth in futility. We must
act for ourselves; is not this the free will and indepen-
dence men claim as their basic right? So join us in killing
this ravenous beast."

Ixon Myrex held up his hands, which trembled with
indignation. "Return the kragen to the lagoon, that thereby—"

"That thereby it may destroy more arbors?" demanded Sklar Hast. "This is not the result I hope for. Nor
do you offer the support you might. Who is more important—the men of the Floats or the kragen?"

This argument struck a chord in his comrades, and
they all shouted: "Yes, who is more important—men or
kragen?"

"Men rule the floats, King Kragen rules the ocean,"

stated Ixon Myrex. "There is no question of comparing importances."

"The lagoon is also under the jurisdiction of man," said Sklar Hast. "This particular kragen is now on the float. Where is the rope?"

Arbiter Myrex called out in his sternest tones: "This is how I interpret the customs of Tranque Float: The kragen must be restored to the water, with all haste. No other course is consistent with custom."

There was a stirring among the men who had helped snare the sea-beast. Sklar Hast said nothing, but taking up the rope, formed a noose. He crawled forward, flipped up the noose to catch a dangling vane, then crawling back and rising to his feet, he circled the creature, binding the dangling vanes. The kragen's motions became increasingly constricted and finally were reduced to spasmodic shudders. Sklar Hast approached the creature from the rear, careful to remain out of reach of mandibles and palps, and made the bonds secure. "Now —the vile beast can only squirm. Lower it to the pad, and we will find a means to make its end."

The guy ropes were shifted; the pole tilted and swung; the kragen fell to the surface of the pad, where it lay passive, palps and mandibles moving slightly in and out. It showed no agitation or discomfort; perhaps it felt none. The exact degree of the kragen's sensitivity and ratiocinative powers had never been determined.

In the east the sky was lightening where the cluster of flaring blue and white suns known as Phocan's Cauldron began to rise. The ocean glimmered with a leaden sheen, and the folk who stood on the central pad began to glance furtively along the obscure horizon, muttering and complaining. Some few called out encouragement to Sklar Hast, recommending the most violent measures against the kragen. Between these and others furious arguments raged. Zander Rohan stood by Ixon Myrex, both obviously disapproving of Sklar Hast's activity. Of the Caste Elders only Poe Belrod and Elmar Pronave, Jackleg and Master Withe-weaver, defended Sklar Hast and his unconventional acts.

Sklar Hast ignored all. He sat watching the black hulk with vast distaste, furious with himself as well for having become involved in so perilous a project. What, after all, had been gained? The kragen had broken his arbors; he had revenged himself and prevented more destruction; well enough, but he had also incurred the ill will of the most influential folk of the float. More seriously, he had involved those others who had trusted him and looked to him for leadership and toward whom he now felt responsibility.

He rose to his feet. There was no help for it; the sooner the beast was disposed of, the more quickly life would return to normal. He approached the kragen, examined it gingerly. The mandibles quivered in their anxiety to sever Sklar Hast's torso; Sklar stayed warily to the side. How to kill the beast?

Elmar Pronave approached, the better to examine the creature. He was a tall man with a high-bridged broken nose and black hair worn in the two ear-plumes of the old Procurer Caste, now no longer in existence save for a few aggressively unique individuals scattered through the floats, who used the caste-marks to emphasize their emotional detachment.

Pronave circled the hulk, kicked at the rear vane, bent to peer into one of the staring eyes. "If we could cut it up, the parts might be of some use."

"The hide is too tough for our knives," growled Sklar Hast. "There's no neck to be strangled."

"There are other ways to kill."

Sklar Hast nodded. "We could sink the beast into the depths of the ocean—but what to use for weight? Bones? Far too valuable. We could load bags with ash, but there is not that much ash to hand. We could burn every hut on the float, as well as the hoodwink tower, and still not secure sufficient. To burn the kragen would require a like mountain of fuel."

A young Larcener who had worked with great enthusiasm during the trapping of the kragen spoke forth: "Poison exists! Find me poison, I will fix a capsule to a stick and push it into the creature's maw!"

Elmar Pronave gave a sardonic bark of laughter. "Agreed; poisons exist, hundreds of them, derived from various sea-plants and animals—but which are sufficiently acrid to destroy this beast? And where is it to be had? I doubt if there is that much poison nearer than Lamp Float."

Phocan's Cauldron, rising into the sky, revealed the kragen in fuller detail. Sklar Hast examined the four blind-seeming eyes in the turret, the intricate construction of the mandibles and tentacles at the maw. He touched the turret, peered at the dome-shaped cap of chitin that covered it. The turret itself seemed laminated, as if constructed of sacked rings of cartilage, the eyes protruding fore and aft in inflexible tubes of rugose harsh substance.

Others in the group began to crowd close; Sklar Hast jumped forward, thrust at a young Felon boat-builder, but too late. The kragen flung out a palp, seized the youth around the neck. Sklar Hast cursed, heaved, tore; the clenched palp was unyielding. Another curled out for his leg; Sklar Hast kicked, danced back, still heaving upon the felon's writhing form.

The kragen drew the felon slowly forward, hoping, so Sklar Hast realized, to pull him within easier reach. He loosened his grip, but the kragen allowed its palp to sway back to encourage Sklar Hast, who once more tore at the constricting member.

Again the kragen craftily drew its captive and Sklar Hast forward; the second palp snapped out once more and this time coiled around Sklar Hast's leg. Sklar Hast dropped to the ground, twisted himself around and broke the hold, though losing skin. The kragen petulantly jerked the felon to within reach of its mandible, snipped off the young man's head, tossed body and head aside.

A horrified gasp came from the watching crowd. Ixon Myrex bellowed, "Sklar Hast, a man's life is gone, due to your savage obstinacy! You have much to answer for! Woe to you!"

Sklar Hast ignored the imprecation. He ran to the warehouse, found chisels and a mallet with a head of dense sea-plant stem, brought up from a depth of two hundred feet.* The chisels had blades of pelvic bone ground sharp against a board gritted with the silica husks of foraminifera. Sklar Hast returned to the kragen, put the chisel against the pale lamellum between the chitin dome and the foliations of the turret. He tapped; the chisel penetrated; this, the substance of a new layer being added to the turret, was relatively soft, the consistency of cooked gristle. Sklar Hast struck again; the chisel cut deep. The kragen squirmed.

Sklar Hast worked the chisel back out, made a new incision beside the first, then another and another, working around the periphery of the chitin dome, which was approximately two feet in diameter. The kragen squirmed and shuddered, whether in pain or apprehension it alone knew. As Sklar Hast worked around to the front, the palps groped back for him, but he shielded himself behind the turret and finally gouged out the lamellum completely around the circumference of the turret.

His followers watched in awe and silence; from the others who watched came somber mutters, and occasional whimpers of superstitious dread from the children.

The channel was cut; Sklar Hast handed chisel and mallet back to Elmar Pronave. He mounted the body of the kragen, bent his knees, hooked fingers under the edge of the chitin dome, heaved. The dome ripped up and off, almost unbalancing Sklar Hast. The dome rolled down to the pad, the turret stood like an open-topped cylinder; within were coils and loops of something like dirty gray string. There were knots here, nodes there, on each side a pair of kinks, to the front a great tangle of kinks and loops.

---

*The advertiserman takes below a pulley which he attaches to a sea-plant stalk. By means of ropes, buckets of air are pulled down, allowing him to remain under water as long as he chooses. Using two such systems, alternately lowered, the diver can descend to a depth of two hundred feet, where the sea-plant stalks grow dense and rigid.

Sklar Hast looked down in interest. He was joined by
Elmar Pronave. "The creature's brain, evidently," said
Sklar Hast. "Here the ganglions terminate. Or perhaps
they are merely the termini of muscles."

Elmar Pronave took the mallet and with the handle
prodded at a node. The kragen gave a furious jerk.
"Well, well," said Pronave. "Interesting indeed." He
prodded further, here, there. Every time he touched the
exposed ganglions, the kragen jerked. Sklar Hast suddenly put out his hand to halt him. "Notice. On the right,
those two long loops; likewise on the left. When you
touched this one here, the fore-vane jerked." He took
the mallet, prodded each of the loops in turn, and in turn
each of the vanes jerked.

"Aha!" declared Elmar Pronave. "Should we persist,
we could teach the kragen to jig."

"Best we should kill the beast," said Sklar Hast. "Dawn
is approaching, and who knows but what . . ." From the
float sounded a sudden low wail, quickly cut off as by the
constriction of breath. The group around the kragen
stirred; someone vented a deep sound of dismay. Sklar
Hast jumped up on the kragen, looked around. The
population on the float were staring out to sea; he looked
likewise, to see King Kragen.

King Kragen floated under the surface, only his turret
above water. The eyes stared forward, each a foot across:
lenses of tough crystal behind which flickered milky
films and a pale blue sheen. King Kragen had either
drifted close down the trail of Phocan's Cauldron on the
water or had approached subsurface.

Fifty feet from the lagoon nets he let his bulk come to
the surface: first the whole of his turret, then the
black cylinder housing the maw and the digestive process, finally the great flat sub-body: this, five feet thick,
thirty feet wide, sixty feet long. To the sides protruded
propulsive vanes, thick as the girth of three men. Viewed
from dead ahead, King Kragen appeared a deformed
ogre swimming the breast-stroke. His forward eyes, in
their horn tubes, were turned toward the float of Sklar
Hast and seemed fixed upon the hulk of the mutilated

kragen. The men stared back, muscles stiff as sea-plant stalk. The kragen which they had captured, once so huge and formidable, now seemed a miniature, a doll, a toy. Through its after-eyes it saw King Kragen and gave a fluting whistle, a sound completely lost and desolate.

Sklar Hast suddenly found his tongue. He spoke in a husky, urgent tone. "Back. To the back of the float."

Now rose the voice of Semm Voiderveg the Intercessor. In quavering tones he called out across the water. "Behold, King Kragen, the men of Tranque Float! Now we denounce the presumptuous bravado of these few heretics! Behold, this pleasant lagoon, with its succulent sponges, devoted to the well-being of the magnanimous King Kragen—" The reedy voice faltered as King Kragen twitched his great vanes and eased forward. The great eyes stared without discernible expression, but behind there seemed to be a leaping and shifting of pale pink and blue lights. The folk on the float drew back as King Kragen breasted close to the net. With a twitch of his vanes, he ripped the net; two more twitches shredded it. From the folk on the float came a moan of dread; King Kragen had not been mollified.

King Kragen eased into the lagoon, approached the helpless kragen. The bound beast thrashed feebly, sounded its fluting whistle. King Kragen reached forth a palp, seized it, lifted it into the air, where it dangled helplessly. King Kragen drew it contemptuously close to his great mandibles, chopped it quickly into slices of gray and black gristle. These he tossed away, out into the ocean. He paused to drift a moment, to consider. Then he surged on Sklar Hast's pad. One blow of his fore-vane demolished the hut, another cut a great gouge in the pad. The after-vanes thrashed among the arbors; water, debris, broken sponges boiled up from below. King Kragen thrust again, wallowed completely up on the pad, which slowly crumpled and sank beneath his weight.

King Kragen pulled himself back into the lagoon, cruised back and forth destroying arbors, shredding the net, smashing huts of all the pads of the lagoon. Then he turned his attention to the main float, breasting up to the edge. For a moment he eyed the population, which started to set up a terrified keening sound, then thrust himself forward, wallowed up on the float, and the keening became a series of hoarse cries and screams. The folk ran back and forth with jerky, scurrying steps.

King Kragen bulked on the float like a toad on a lily pad. He struck with his vanes; the float split. The hoodwink tower, the great structure so cunningly woven, so carefully contrived, tottered. King Kragen lunged again, the tower toppled, falling into the huts along the north edge of the float.

King Kragen floundered across the float. He destroyed the granary, and bushels of yellow meal laboriously scraped from sea-plant pistils streamed into the water. He crushed the racks where stalk, withe, and fiber were stretched and flexed; he dealt likewise with the rope-walk. Then, as if suddenly in a hurry, he swung about, heaved himself to the southern edge of the float. A number of huts and thirty-two of the folk, mostly aged or very young, were crushed or thrust into the water and drowned.

King Kragen regained the open sea. He floated quietly a moment or two, palps twitching in the expression of some unknowable emotion. Then he moved his vanes and slid off across the calm ocean.

Tranque Float was a devastation, a tangle, a scene of wrath and grief. The lagoon had returned to the ocean, with the arbors reduced to rubbish and the shoals of food-fish scattered. Many huts had been crushed. The hoodwink tower lay toppled. Of a population of four-hundred and eighty, forty-three were dead, with as many more injured. The survivors stood blank-eyed and limp, unable to comprehend the full extent of the disaster that had come upon them.

Presently they roused themselves and gathered at the far western edge, where the damage had been the least. Ixon Myrex sought through the faces, eventually spied Sklar Hast sitting on a fragment of the fallen hoodwink tower. He raised his hand slowly, pointed. "Sklar

Hast! I denounce you! The evil you have done to Tranque Float cannot be uttered in words. Your arrogance,
your callous indifference to our pleas, your cruel and
audacious villainy—how can you hope to expiate them?"

Sklar Hast paid no heed. His attention was fixed upon
Meril Rohan, where she knelt beside the body of Zander
Rohan, his fine brisk mop of white hair dark with blood.

Ixon Myrex called in a harsh voice: "In my capacity
as Arbiter of Tranque Float, I declare you a criminal of
the basest sort, together with all those who served you
as accomplices, and most noteworthy Elmar Pronave!
Elmar Pronave, show your shameful face! Where do you
hide?"

But Elmar Pronave had been drowned and did not
answer.

Ixon Myrex returned to Sklar Hast. "The Master Hoodwink is dead and cannot denounce you in his own terms.
I will speak for him: you are Assistant Master Hoodwink no longer. You are ejected from your caste and
your calling!"

Sklar Hast wearily gave his attention to Ixon Myrex.
"Do not bellow nonsense. You can eject me from nothing. I am Master Hoodwink now. I was Master Hoodwink
as soon as I bested Zander Rohan; even had I not done
so, I became Master Hoodwink upon his death. You outrank me not an iota; you can denounce but do no more."

Semm Voiderveg the Intercessor spoke forth. "Denunciations are not enough! Argument in regard to rank
is footling! King Kragen, in wreaking his terrible but
just vengeance, intended that the primes of the deed
should die. I now declare the will of King Kragen to be
death, by either strangulation or bludgeoning, for Sklar
Hast and all his accomplices."

"Not so fast," said Sklar Hast. "It appears to me that
a certain confusion is upon us. Two kragen, a large one
and a small one, have injured us. I, Sklar Hast, and my
friends, are those who hoped to protect the float from
depredation. We failed. We are not criminals; we are
simply not as strong or as wicked as King Kragen."

"Are you aware," thundered Semm Voiderveg, "that King Kragen reserves to himself the duty of guarding us from the lesser kragen? Are you aware that in assaulting the kragen, you in effect assaulted King Kragen?"

Sklar Hast considered. "I am aware that we will need more powerful tools than ropes and chisels to kill King Kragen."

Semm Voiderveg turned away, speechless. The people looked apathetically toward Sklar Hast. Few seemed to share the indignation of the elders.

Ixon Myrex sensed the general feeling of misery and fatigue. "This is no time for recrimination. There is work to be done." His voice broke with his own deep and sincere grief. "All our fine structures must be rebuilt, our tower rendered operative, our net rewoven." He stood quiet for a moment, and something of his rage returned. "Sklar Hast's crime must not go without appropriate punishment. I ordain a Grand Convocation to take place in three days, on Apprise Float. The fate of Sklar Hast and his gang will be decided by a Council of Elders."

Sklar Hast walked away. He approached Meril Rohan, who sat with her face in her hands, tears streaming down her cheeks.

"I'm sorry that your father died," said Sklar Hast awkwardly. "I'm sorry anyone died—but I'm especially sorry that you should be hurt."

Meril Rohan surveyed him with an expression he was unable to decipher. He spoke in a voice hardly more than a husky mutter. "Someday the sufferings of the Tranque folk must lead to a happier future—for all the folk, of all the floats.... I see it is my destiny to kill King Kragen. I care for nothing else."

Meril Rohan spoke in a clear, quiet voice. "I wish my duty were as plain to me. I, too, must do something. I must expunge or help to expunge whatever has caused this evil that today has come upon us. Is it King Kragen? Is it Sklar Hast? Or something else altogether?" She was musing now, her eyes unfocused, almost as if she were unaware of her father's corpse, of Sklar Hast stand-

ing before her. "It is a fact that the evil exists. The evil
has a source. So my problem is to locate the source of
the evil, to learn its nature. Only when we know our
enemy can we defeat it."

Chapter 4

The ocean had never been plumbed. At two hundred feet the maximum depth attempted by stalk-cutters and pod-gatherers, the sea-plant stems were still a tangle. One Ben Murmen, Sixth, an Advertiserman, half-daredevil, half-maniac, had descended to three hundred feet, and in the indigo gloom noted the stalks merging to disappear into the murk as a single great trunk. But attempts to sound the bottom, by means of a line weighted with a bag of bone chippings, were unsuccessful. How, then, had the sea-plants managed to anchor themselves? Some supposed that the plants were of great antiquity and had developed during a time when the water was much lower. Others conjectured a sinking of the ocean bottom; still others were content to ascribe the feat to an innate tendency of the sea-plants.

Of all the floats, Apprise was the largest and one of the first to be settled. The central agglomeration was perhaps nine acres in extent; the lagoon was bounded by thirty or forty smaller pads. Apprise Float was the traditional site of the convocations, which occurred at approximately yearly intervals and which were attended by the active and responsible adults of the system, who seldom otherwise ventured far from home, since it was widely believed that King Kragen disapproved of travel. He ignored the coracles of swindlers, and also the rafts of withe or stalk which occasionally passed between the floats, but on other occasions he had demolished boats or coracles that had no ostensible business or purpose.

53

Coracles conveying folk to a convocation had never
been molested, however, even though King Kragen always
seemed aware that a convocation was in progress, and
often watched proceedings from a distance of a quarter-
mile or so. How King Kragen gained his knowledge was
a matter of great mystery; some asserted that on every
float lived a man who was a man in semblance only,
who inwardly was a manifestation of King Kragen. It
was through this man, according to the superstition, that
King Kragen knew what transpired on the floats.

For three days preceding the convocation there was
incessant flickering along the line of the hoodwink towers;
the destruction of Tranque Float was reported in full detail, together with Ixon Myrex's denunciation of Sklar
Hast and Sklar Hast's rebuttal. On each of the floats there
was intense discussion and a certain degree of debate.
Since, in most cases, the arbiter and the intercessor of
each float inveighed against Sklar Hast, there was little
organized sentiment in his favor.

On the morning of the convocation, early, before the
morning sky showed blue, coracles full of folk moved between the floats. The survivors of the Tranque Float disaster, who for the most part had sought refuge on
Thrasneck and Bickle, were among the first under way,
as were the folk from Almack and Sciona, in the far
west.

All morning the coracles shuttled back and forth between the floats; shortly before noon the first groups began to arrive on Apprise. Each group wore the distinctive
emblems of its float, and those who felt caste distinction
important likewise wore the traditional hair-stylings,
forehead plaques, and dorsal ribbons; otherwise all
dressed in much the same fashion: shirts and pantalets
of coarse linen woven from sea-plant fiber, sandals of
rug-fish leather, ceremonial gauntlets and epaulettes of
sequins cut from the kernels of a certain half-animal,
half-vegetable mollusk.

As the folk arrived, they trooped to the famous old Apprise Inn where they refreshed themselves at a table
on which was set forth a collation of beer, pod-cakes,

pepperfish, and pickled fingerlings, after which the newcomers separated to various quarters of the float, in accordance with traditional caste distinctions.

In the center of the float was a rostrum. On surrounding benches the notables took their places: craft-masters, caste-elders, arbiters and intercessors. The rostrum was at all times open to any person who wished to speak, so long as he gained the sponsorship of one of the notables. The first speakers at the convocations customarily were elders intent on exhorting the younger folk to excellence and virtue; so it was today. An hour after the sun had reached the zenith, the first speaker made his way to the rostrum—a portly old Incendiary from Maudelinda Float who had in just such a fashion opened the speaking at the last five convocations. He sought and was perfunctorily granted sponsorship—by now his speeches were regarded as a necessary evil. He mounted the rostrum and began to speak. His voice was rich, throbbing, voluminous; his periods were long, his sentiments well-used, his illuminations unremarkable.

"We meet again. I am pleased to see so many of the faces which over the years have become familiar and well-beloved, and alas there are certain faces no more to be seen, those who have slipped away to the Bourne, many untimely, as those who suffered punishment only these few days past before the wrath of King Kragen, of whom we all stand in awe. A dreadful circumstance thus to provoke the majesty of this Elemental Reality; it should never have occurred; it would never have occurred if all abided by the ancient disciplines. Why must we scorn the wisdom of our ancestors? Those noble and most heroic of men who dared revolt against the tyranny of the mindless helots, to seize the Ship of Space which was taking them to brutal confinement, and to seek a haven here on this blessed world! Our ancestors knew the benefits of order and rigor; they designated the castes and set them to tasks for which they presumably had received training on the Home World. In such a fashion the Swindlers were assigned the task of swindling fish; the Hoodwinks were set to winking hoods; the Incendiaries, among whom I 'am proud to number myself, wove ropes; while the Bezzlers gave us many of the intercessors who have procured the favor and benevolent guardianship of King Kragen.

"Like begets like; characteristics persist and distill. Why, then, are the castes crumbling and giving way to helter-skelter disorder? I appeal to the youth of today: read the Analects; study the artifacts in the Museum; renew your dedication to the system formulated by our forefathers. You have no heritage more precious than your caste identity!"

The old Incendiary spoke on in such a vein for several minutes further and was succeeded by another old man, a former Hoodwink of good reputation, who worked until films upon his eyes gave one configuration much the look of another. Like the old Incendiary, he, too, urged a more fervent dedication to the old-time values. "I deplore the sloth of today's youth! We are becoming a race of sluggards! It is sheer good fortune that King Kragen protects us from the gluttony of the lesser kragen. And what if the tyrants of out-space discovered our haven and sought once more to enslave us? How would we defend ourselves? By hurling fish-heads? By diving under the floats in the hope that our adversaries would follow and drown themselves? I propose that each float form a militia, well-trained and equipped with darts and spears, fashioned from the hardest and most durable stalk obtainable!"

The old Hoodwink was followed by the Sumber Float Intercessor, who courteously suggested that should the out-space tyrants appear, King Kragen would be sure to visit upon them the most poignant punishments, the most absolute of rebuffs, so that the tyrants would flee in terror, never to return. "King Kragen is mighty, King Kragen is wise and benevolent, unless his dignity is impugned, as in the detestable incident at Tranque Float, where the willfulness of a bigoted freethinker caused agony to many." Now he modestly turned down his head. "It is neither my place nor my privilege to propose a punishment suitable to so heinous an offense as the one under discussion. But I would go beyond this particular crime to dwell upon the underlying causes; namely the bravado of certain folk, who ordain themselves equal or superior to the accepted ways of life which have served us so well so long . . . ."

Presently he descended to the float. His place was taken by a somber man of stalwart physique, wearing the plainest of garments. "My name is Sklar Hast," he said. "I am that so-called bigoted freethinker just referred to. I have much to say, but I hardly know how to say it. I will be blunt. King Kragen is not the wise, beneficent guardian the intercessors like to pretend. King Kragen is a gluttonous beast who every year becomes more enormous and more gluttonous. I sought to kill a lesser kragen which I found destroying my arbors; by some means King Kragen learned of this attempt and reacted with insane malice."

"Hist! Hist!" cried the intercessors from below. "Shame! Outrage!"

"Why does King Kragen resent my effort? After all, he kills any lesser kragen he discovers in the vicinity. It is simple and self-evident. King Kragen does not want men to think about killing kragen for fear they will attempt to kill him. I propose that this is what we do. Let us put aside this ignoble servility, this groveling to a sea-beast, let us turn our best efforts to the destruction of King Kragen."

"Irresponsible maniac!" "Fool!" "Vile-minded ingrate!" called the intercessors.

Sklar Hast waited, but the invective increased in volume. Finally Phyral Berwick, the Apprise Arbiter, mounted the rostrum and held up his hands. "Quiet! Let Sklar Hast speak! He stands on the rostrum; it is his privilege to say what he wishes."

"Must we listen to garbage and filth?" called Semm Voiderveg. "This man has destroyed Tranque Float; now he urges his frantic lunacy upon everyone else."

"Let him urge," declared Phyral Berwick. "You are under no obligation to comply."

Sklar Hast said, "The intercessors naturally resist these

ideas; they are bound closely to King Kragen and claim
to have some means of communicating with him. Possibly
this is so. Why else should King Kragen arrive so oppor-
tunely at Tranque Float? Now here is a very cogent
point: if we can agree to liberate ourselves from King
Kragen, we must prevent the intercessors from making
known our plans to him—otherwise we shall suffer more
than necessary. Most of you know in your hearts that
I speak truth. King Kragen is a crafty beast with an in-
satiable appetite, and we are his slaves. You know this
truth, but you fear to acknowledge it. Those who spoke
before me have mentioned our forefathers: the men who
captured a ship from the tyrants who sought to immure
them on a penal planet. What would our forefathers
have done? Would they have submitted to this gluttonous ogre? Of course not.

"How can we kill King Kragen? The plans must wait
upon agreement, upon the concerted will to act, and in
any event must not be told before the intercessors. If
there are any here who believe as I do, now is the time
for them to make themselves heard."

He stepped down from the rostrum. Across the float
was silence. Men's faces were frozen. Sklar Hast looked
to right and to left. No one met his eye.

The portly Semm Voiderveg mounted the rostrum.
"You have listened to the murderer. He knows no shame.
On Tranque Float we condemned him to death for his
malevolent acts. According to custom he demanded the
right to speak before a convocation; now he has done
so. Has he confessed his great crime? Has he wept for
the evil he has visited upon Tranque Float? No! He gib-
bers his plans for further enormities; he outrages de-
cency by mentioning our ancestors in the same breath
with his foul proposals! Let the convocation endorse the
verdict of Tranque Float; let all those who respect King
Kragen and benefit from his ceaseless vigilance raise
now their hands in the clenched fist of death!"

"Death!" roared the intercessors and raised their fists.
But elsewhere through the crowd there was hesitation

and uneasiness. Eyes shifted backward and forward; there were furtive glances out to sea.

Semm Voiderveg looked back and forth across the crowd in disappointment. "I well understand your reluctance to visit violence upon a fellowman, but in this case any squeamishness whatever is misplaced." He pointed a long, pale finger at Sklar Hast. "Do you understand the pure, concentrated villainy embodied in this man? I will expatiate. Just prior to the offense for which he is on trial, he committed another, against his benefactor and superior, Master Hoodwink Zander Rohan. But this furtive act, this attempt to cheat the Master Hoodwink in a winking contest and thus dislodge the noble Rohan from his office, was detected by Tranque Arbiter Ixon Myrex and myself, and so failed to succeed."

Sklar Hast roared: "What? Is there no protection from slander here? Must I submit to venom of this sort?"

Phyral Berwick told him, "Your recourse is simple. You may let the man speak, then if you can prove slander, the slanderer must face an appropriate penalty."

Semm Voiderveg spoke with great earnestness. "Mind you, a harsh truth is not slander. Personal malice must be proved as a motive. And there is no reason why I should feel malice. To continue—"

But Sklar Hast appealed to Phyral Berwick. "Before he continues, I feel that the matter of slander should be clarified. I wish to prove that this man accuses me from spite."

"Can you do so?"

"Yes."

"Very well." Phyral Berwick motioned to Semm Voiderveg. "You must delay the balance of your remarks until the matter of slander is settled."

"You need only request information of Arbiter Myrex," protested Semm Voiderveg. "He will assure you that the facts are as I have stated."

Phyral Berwick nodded to Sklar Hast. "Proceed: prove slander, if you can."

Sklar Hast pointed to Second Assistant Hoodwink Vick Caverbee. "Please stand forth."

Caverbee, a small sandy-haired man with a wry face, his nose slanted in one direction, mouth in another, stepped somewhat reluctantly forward. Sklar Hast said, "Voiderveg claims that I outwinked Master Hoodwink Rohan by means of diligent practice of the test exercises. Is this true?"

"No. It's not true. It can't possibly be true. The apprentices have been training on Exercises one through fifty. When Arbiter Myrex asked for exercises to be used for the contest, I brought the advanced exercises from the locker. He and Intercessor Voiderveg made the selection themselves."

Sklar Hast pointed to Arbiter Myrex. "True or false?"

Arbiter Myrex drew a deep breath. "True, in a technical sense. Still, you had an opportunity to practice the exercises."

"So did Master Hoodwink Rohan," said Sklar Hast with a grim smile. "Needless to say, I did nothing of the sort."

"So much is clear," said Phyral Berwick curtly. "But as for slander—"

Sklar Hast nodded toward Caverbee. "He has the answer for that also."

Caverbee spoke even more reluctantly than before. "Intercessor Voiderveg wished to espouse the Master Hoodwink's daughter. He spoke of the matter first to the Master Hoodwink, then to Meril Rohan. I could not help but overhear the matter. She gave him a flat refusal. The Intercessor asked the reason, and Meril Rohan said that she planned to espouse the Assistant Hoodwink Sklar Hast, if ever he approached her as if she were something other than a kick-release on a wink machine. Intercessor Voiderveg seemed very much annoyed."

"Bah!" called Voiderveg, his face flaming pink. "What of slander now?"

Sklar Hast looked through the crowd. His eyes met those of Meril Rohan. She did not wait to be requested to speak. She rose to her feet. "I am Meril Rohan. The evidence of the Second Assistant Hoodwink is by and large accurate. At that time I planned to espouse Sklar Hast."

Sklar Hast turned back to Phyral Berwick. "There is the evidence."

"You have made a reasonable case. I adjudicate that Intercessor Semm Voiderveg is guilty of slander. What penalty do you demand?"

"None. It is a trivial matter. I merely want the issues judged on the merits, without the extraneous factors brought forward by Intercessor Voiderveg."

Phyral Berwick turned to Voiderveg. "You may continue speaking, but you must refrain from further slander."

"I will say no more," said Voiderveg in a thick voice. "Eventually I will be vindicated." He stepped down from the rostrum, marched over to sit beside Arbiter Myrex, who somewhat pointedly ignored him.

A tall dark-haired man wearing a richly detailed gown of white, scarlet, and black, asked for the rostrum. This was Barquan Blasdel, Apprise Intercessor. He had a sobriety, an ease, a dignity of manner that lent him vastly more conviction than that exercised by the somewhat over-fervid Semm Voiderveg.

"As the accused admits, the matter of slander is remote to the case, and I suggest that we dismiss it utterly from our minds. Aside from this particular uncertainty, none other exists. The issues are stark—almost embarrassingly clear. The Covenant requires that King Kragen be accorded the justice of the sea. Sklar Hast wantonly, deliberately, and knowingly violated the Covenant and brought about the death of forty-three men and women. There can be no argument." Barquan Blasdel shrugged in a deprecatory manner. "Much as I dislike to ask the death penalty, I must. So fists high then! Death to Sklar Hast!"

"Death!" roared the intercessors once again, holding high their fists, turning around and gesturing to others in the throng to join them.

Barquan Blasdel's temperate exposition swayed more folk than Voiderveg's accusations, but still there was a sense of hesitation, of uncertainty, as if all suspected that there was yet more to be said.

Barquan Blasdel leaned quizzically forward over the rostrum. "What? You are reluctant in so clear a case? I cannot prove more than I have."

Phyral Berwick, the Apprise Arbiter, rose to his feet. "I remind Barquan Blasdel that he has now called twice for the death of Sklar Hast. If he calls once more and fails to achieve an affirmative vote, Sklar Hast is vindicated."

Barquan Blasdel smiled out over the crowd. He turned a swift, almost furtive look of appraisal toward Sklar Hast and without further statement descended to the float.

The rostrum was empty. No one sought to speak. Finally Phyral Berwick himself mounted the steps: a stocky, square-faced man with gray hair, ice-blue eyes, a short gray beard. He spoke slowly. "Sklar Hast calls for the death of King Kragen. Semm Voiderveg and Barquan Blasdel call for the death of Sklar Hast. I will tell you my feelings. I have great fear in the first case and great disinclination in the second. I have no clear sense of what I should do. Sklar Hast, rightly or wrongly, has forced us to a decision. We should consider with care and make no instant judgments."

Barquan Blasdel jumped to his feet. "Respectfully I must urge that we hold to the issue under consideration, and this is the degree of Sklar Hast's guilt in connection with the Tranque Float tragedy."

Phyral Berwick gave a curt nod. "We will recess for an hour."

Chapter 5

Sklar Hast pushed through the crowd to where he had seen Meril Rohan, but when he reached the spot, she had moved away. As he stood searching for her, men and women of various floats, castes, guilds, and generations pressed forward to stare at him, to speak to him, tentatively, curiously. A few, motivated by a psychic morbidity, reached out to touch him; a few reviled him in hoarse, choked voices. A tall red-haired man, of the Peculator caste by his artfully dyed emblem of five colors, thrust forward an excited face. "You speak of killing King Kragen—how may this be done?"

Sklar Hast said in a careful voice, "I don't know. But I hope to learn."

"And if King Kragen becomes infuriated by your hostility and ravages each of the floats in turn?"

"There might be temporary suffering, but our children and their children would benefit."

Another spoke: a short clench-jawed woman. "If it means my toil and my suffering and my death, I would as soon that these misfortunes be shared by those who would benefit."

"All this is a personal matter, of course," said Sklar Hast politely. He attempted to sidle away, but was halted by another woman, this one wearing the blue and white sash of Hooligan Preceptress, who shook her finger under the first woman's nose. "What of the Two Hundred who fled the tyrants? Do you think they worried about risk? No! They sacrificed all to avoid slavery, and we have benefited. Are we immune then from danger and sacrifice?"

"No!" shouted the first woman. "But we need not urge it upon ourselves!"

An intercessor from one of the outer floats stepped forward. "King Kragen is our benefactor! What is this foolish talk of risk and slavery and sacrifice? Instead we should speak of gratitude and praise and worship."

The red-haired Peculator, leaning in front of Sklar Hast, waved his arms impatiently at the intercessor: "Why don't the intercessors and all of like mind take King Kragen and voyage to a far float and serve him as they please, but leave the remainder of us in peace?"

"King Kragen serves us all," declared the intercessor with great dignity. "We would be performing an ignoble act to deprive everyone else of his beneficent guardianship."

The Hooligan Preceptress had a countering remark, but Sklar Hast managed to step aside, and now he saw Meril Rohan at a nearby booth, where she sipped tea from a mug. He edged through the crowd and joined her. She acknowledged his presence with the coolest of nods.

"Come," said Sklar Hast, taking her arm. "Let us move to the side, where the folk do not crush in on us. I have much to say to you."

"I don't care to talk with you. A display of childish petulance perhaps, but this is the situation."

"And it is precisely what I wish to discuss with you," declared Sklar Hast.

Meril Rohan smiled faintly. "Better that you be contriving arguments to save your neck. The convocation may well decide that your life has continued as long as is desirable."

Sklar Hast winced. "And how will you vote?"

"I am bored with the entire proceedings. I will probably return to Quatrefoil."

Perceiving the situation to be awkward, Sklar Hast departed with as good grace as he could muster.

He went to join Rubal Gallager, who sat under the Apprise Inn pergola. "The float is in ruins, you have made enemies—still your life is no longer in danger," said Rubal Gallager. "At least this is my opinion."

Sklar Hast gave a sour grunt. "Sometimes I wonder if the effort is worthwhile. Still, there is much to do. If nothing else, the hoodwink tower must be rebuilt. And I have my office to consider."

Rubal Gallager gave a ripe chuckle. "With Semm Voiderveg as Intercessor and Ixon Myrex as Arbiter, your tenure will hardly be one of sheer harmony."

"The least of my worries," said Sklar Hast. "Assuming, of course, that I leave the convocation alive."

"I think you may count upon this," said Rubal Gallager with a somewhat grim overtone to his voice. "There are many who wish you dead, doubtless—but there are many who do not."

Sklar Hast considered a moment and gave his head a dubious shake. "I hardly know what to say. For twelve generations the folk of the floats have lived in harmony, and we think it savage if a man so much as threatens another man with his fist . . . . Would I want to be the node of contention? Would I want the name Sklar Hast to be echoed down the generations as the man who brought strife to the floats?"

Rubal Gallager regarded him in quizzical amusement. "I have never known you previously to wax philosophical."

"It is not an occupation I enjoy," said Sklar Hast, "though it seems as if more and more it is to be forced upon me." He looked across the float to the refreshment booth where Meril Rohan sat speaking across a bench with one who was a stranger to Sklar Hast: a thin young man with an intense, abrupt, angled face and a habit of nervous gesticulation. He wore neither caste nor guild emblems, but from the green piping at the throat of his smock Sklar Hast deduced him to be from Sankston Float.

His thoughts were interrupted by the return of Phyral Berwick to the rostrum.

"We will now resume our considerations. I hope that all who speak will eschew excitement and emotion. This is a deliberative assembly of reasonable and calm beings, not a mob of fanatics to be incited, and I wish all to remember this. If angry men shout at each other, the purpose of the convocation is defeated, and I will again call a recess. So now, who wishes to speak?"

From the audience a man called: "Question!"

Phyral Berwick pointed his finger. "Step forward, state your name, caste, craft, and propound your question."

It was the thin-faced young man with the intense expression whom Sklar Hast had observed speaking with Meril Rohan. He said, "My name is Roger Kelso. My lineage is Larcener, although I have departed from caste custom and my craft now is scrivener. My question has this background: Sklar Hast is accused of responsibility for the Tranque Float disaster, and it is the duty of the convocation to measure this responsibility. To do this we first must measure the proximate cause of tragedy. This is an essential element of traditional jurisprudence, and if any think otherwise, I will quote the Memorium of Lester McManus, where he describes the theoretical elements of Home World law. This is a passage not included in the Analects and is not widely known. Suffice it to say, the man who establishes a precursory condition for a crime is not necessarily guilty; he must actually, immediately, and decisively cause the event."

Barquan Blasdel, in his easy, almost patronizing voice, interrupted: "But this is precisely Sklar Hast's act: he disobeyed King Kragen's statute, and this precipitated his terrible justice."

Roger Kelso listened with a patience obviously foreign to his nature; he fidgeted, and his dark eyes glittered. He said, "If the worthy Intercessor allows, I will continue."

Barquan Blasdel nodded politely and sat down.

"When Sklar Hast spoke, he put forth a conjecture which absolutely must be resolved: namely, did Semm Voiderveg, the Tranque Intercessor, call King Kragen to Tranque Float? This is a subtle question. Much depends upon not only if Semm Voiderveg issued the call, but *when*. If he did so when the rogue kragen was first discovered, well and good. If he called after Sklar Hast made his attempt to kill the kragen, then Semm Voiderveg becomes more guilty of the Tranque disaster than Sklar Hast, because he certainly must have foreseen the consequences. What is the true state of affairs? Do the intercessors secretly communicate with King Kragen? And my specific question: did Semm Voiderveg call King Kragen to Tranque Float in order that Sklar Hast and his helpers be punished?"

"Bah!" called Barquan Blasdel. "This is a diversion, a dialectic trick!"

Phyral Berwick deliberated a moment. "The question seems definite enough. I personally cannot supply an answer, but I think that it deserves one, if only to clarify matters. Semm Voiderveg: what do you say?"

"I say nothing."

"Come," said Phyral Berwick reasonably. "Your craft is Intercessor; your responsibility lies to the men whom you represent and for whom you intercede; certainly not to King Kragen, no matter how fervent your respect. Evasion, secrecy, or stubborn silence can only arouse our distrust and lead away from justice. Surely you recognize this much."

"It is to be understood," said Semm Voiderveg tartly, "that even if I did summon King Kragen—and it would violate guild policy to make a definite statement in this regard—my motives were of the highest order."

"Well, then, did you do so?"

Semm Voiderveg looked toward Barquan Blasdel for support, and the Apprise Intercessor once more rose to his feet. "Arbiter Berwick, I must insist that we are pursuing a blind alley, far from our basic purpose."

"What then is our basic purpose?" asked Phyral Berwick.

Barquan Blasdel held out his arms in a gesture of surprise. "Is there any doubt? By Sklar Hast's own admission he has violated King Kragen's laws and the orthodox custom of the floats. It only remains to us—this and no more—to establish a commensurate punishment."

Phyral Berwick started to speak, but yielded to Roger

Kelso, who had leaped quickly to his feet. "I must point out an elemental confusion in the worthy Intercessor's thinking. King Kragen's laws are not human laws, and is unorthodoxy a crime? If so, then many more beside Sklar Hast are guilty."

Barquan Blasdel remained unruffled. "The confusion lies in another quarter. The laws I refer to stem from the Covenant between ourselves and King Kragen: he protects us from the terrors of the sea; in return he insists that we acknowledge his sovereignty of the sea. And as for orthodoxy, this is no more and no less than respect for the opinions of the arbiters and intercessors of all the floats, who are trained to judiciousness, foresight, and decorum. So now we must weigh the exact degree of Sklar Hast's transgressions."

"Precisely," said Roger Kelso. "And to do this, we need to know whether Semm Voiderveg summoned King Kragen to Tranque Float."

Barquan Blasdel's voice at last took on a harsh edge. "We must not question the acts of any man when he performs in the role of intercessor! Nor is it permitted to probe the guild secrets of the intercessors!"

Phyral Berwick signaled Barquan Blasdel to silence. "In a situation like this, when fundamental questions are under consideration, guild secrecy becomes of secondary importance. Not only I but all the other folk of the floats wish to know the truth, with a minimum of obscurantism. Secrecy of any sort may not be allowed: This is my ruling. So then, Semm Voiderveg, you were asked: Did you summon King Kragen to Tranque Float on the night in question?"

The very air seemed to congeal; every eye turned on Semm Voiderveg. He cleared his throat, raised his eyes to the sky. But he showed no embarrassment in his reply. "The question seems nothing less than ingenuous. How could I function as intercessor without some means of conveying to King Kragen both the extent of our trust and fidelity, likewise the news of emergency when such existed? When the rogue appeared, it was no less than my duty to summon King Kragen. I did so. The means are irrelevant."

Barquan Blasdel nodded in profound approval, almost relief. Phyral Berwick drummed his fingers on the rostrum. Several times he opened his mouth to speak, and each time closed it. Finally he asked, rather lamely, "Are these the only occasions upon which you summon King Kragen?"

Semm Voiderveg made a show of indignation. "Why do you question me? I am Intercessor; the criminal is Sklar Hast!"

"Easy, then; the questions illuminate the extent of the alleged crime. For instance, let me ask this: Do you ever summon King Kragen to feed from your lagoon in order to visit a punishment or a warning upon the folk of your float?"

Semm Voiderveg blinked. "The wisdom of King Kragen is inordinate. He can detect delinquencies; he makes his presence known—"

"Specifically, then, you summoned King Kragen to Tranque Float when Sklar Hast sought to kill the rogue?"

"My acts are not in the balance. I see no reason to answer the question."

Barquan Blasdel rose majestically to his feet. "I was about to remark as much."

"And I!" "And I!" Came from various other intercessors.

Phyral Berwick spoke to the crowd in a troubled voice. "There seems no practical way to determine exactly when Semm Voiderveg called King Kragen. If he did so after Sklar Hast had begun his attack upon the rogue, then in my opinion Semm Voiderveg, the Intercessor, is more immediately responsible for the Tranque disaster than Sklar Hast, and it becomes a travesty to visit any sort of penalty upon Sklar Hast. Unfortunately there seems no way of settling this question."

Poe Belrod, the Advertiserman Elder, rose to his feet and stood looking sidelong toward Semm Voiderveg. "I can shed some light on the situation. I was a witness to all that occurred. When the rogue appeared in the lagoon, Semm Voiderveg went to watch with the others. He did not go apart until after Sklar Hast began to kill the beast. I am sure others will be witness to this; Semm Voiderveg made no attempt to conceal his presence."

Several others who had been at the scene corroborated the testimony of Poe Belrod.

The Apprise Intercessor, Barquan Blasdel, again gained the rostrum. "Arbiter Berwick, I beg that you sedulously keep to the paramount issue. The facts are these: Sklar Hast and his gang committed an act knowingly proscribed both by Tranque Arbiter Ixon Myrex and by Tranque Intercessor Semm Voiderveg. The consequences stemmed from this act; Sklar Hast is inevitably guilty."

"Barquan Blasdel," said Phyral Berwick, "you are Apprise Intercessor. Have you ever summoned King Kragen to Apprise Float?"

"As Semm Voiderveg and I have incessantly pointed out, Sklar Hast is the criminal at the bar, not the conscientious intercessors of the various floats. By no means may Sklar Hast be allowed to evade his punishment. King Kragen is not lightly to be defied! Even though the convocation will not raise their collective fist to smite Sklar Hast, I say that he must die. It is a matter this serious."

Phyral Berwick fixed his pale blue eyes upon Barquan Blasdel. "If the convocation gives Sklar Hast his life, he will not die unless I die before him."

"Nor I!" called Poe Belrod. "Nor I!" This was from Roger Kelso. And now all those men of Tranque Float who had joined Sklar Hast in the killing of the rogue kragen came toward the rostrum, shouting their intention of joining Sklar Hast either in life or death, and with them came others, from various floats.

Barquan Blasdel scrambled up onto the rostrum, held his arms wide, and finally was able to make himself heard. "Before others declare themselves—look out to sea! King Kragen watches, attentive to learn who is loyal and who is faithless!"

The crowd swung about as if one individual. A hundred yards off the float the water swirled lazily around King Kragen's great turret. The crystal eyes pointed like telescopes toward Apprise Float. Presently the turret sank beneath the surface. The blue water roiled, then flowed smooth and featureless.

Sklar Hast stepped forward, started to mount to the rostrum. Barquan Blasdel the Intercessor halted him. "The rostrum must not become a shouting place. Stay till you are summoned!"

But Sklar Hast pushed him aside, went to face the crowd. He pointed toward the smooth ocean. "There you have seen the vile beast, our enemy! Why should we deceive ourselves? Intercessors, arbiters, all of us— let us forget our differences, let us join our crafts and our resources! If we do so, we can evolve a method to kill King Kragen! We are men; why should we abase ourselves before anything whatever?"

Barquan Blasdel threw back his head, aghast. He took a step toward Sklar Hast, as if to seize him, then turned to the audience. "You have heard this madman— twice you have heard him! And also you have observed the vigilance of King Kragen whose force is known to all! Choose therefore—obey either the exhortations of a twitching lunatic or be guided by our ancient trust in the benevolence of mighty King Kragen. There must be a definite resolution to this matter. We can have no half measures! Sklar Hast must die! So now hold high your fists —each and all! Silence the frantic screamings of Sklar Hast! King Kragen is near at hand! Death to Sklar Hast!" He thrust his fist high into the air.

The intercessors followed suit. "Death to Sklar Hast!"

Hesitantly, indecisively, other fists raised, then others and others. Some changed their minds and drew down their fists or thrust them high; some raised their fists only to have others pull them down. Altercations sprang up across the float; the hoarse sound of contention began to make itself heard.

Barquan Blasdel leaned forward in sudden concern, calling for calm. Sklar Hast likewise started to speak, but he desisted—because suddenly words were of no avail. In a bewildering, almost magical shift the placid convocation had become a melee. Men and women tore savagely at each other, screaming, cursing, raging, squealing. Emotion accumulated from childhood, stored and constrained, now exploded; identical fear and hate prompted opposite reactions.

Luckily few weapons were available: clubs of stalk, a bone ax or two, a half dozen stakes, as many knives. Across the float the tide of battle surged, out into the water. Staid Jacklegs and responsible Malpractors sought to drown each other; Advertisermen ignored their low estate and belabored Bezzlers; orthodox Incendiaries kicked, clawed, tore, and bit as furiously as any varnish-besotted Smuggler. While the struggle was at its most intense, King Kragen once more surfaced, this time a quarter-mile to the north, whence he turned his vast, incurious gaze upon the float.

The fighting slowed and dwindled, partly from sheer exhaustion, partly from the efforts of the most responsible, and the combatants were thrust apart. In the lagoon floated half a dozen corpses; on the float lay as many more. Now for the first time it could be seen that those who stood by Sklar Hast were considerably outnumbered, by almost two to one, and also that this group included for the most part the most vigorous and able of the craftsmen, though few of the Masters.

Barquan Blasdel, still on the rostrum, cried out, "A sorry day indeed, a sorry day! Sklar Hast, see the anguish you have brought to the floats!"

Sklar Hast looked at him, panting and haggard with grief. Blood coursed down his face from the slash of a knife; the garments were ripped from his chest. Ignoring Blasdel, he mounted the rostrum and addressed the two groups. "I agree with Barquan Blasdel: this is a sorry day—but let there be no mistake: Men must rule the ocean beast or be ruled! I now return to Tranque Float, where the great damage must be repaired. As Blasdel the Intercessor has said, there is no turning back now. So be it. Let those who want free lives come to Tranque, where we will take counsel on what to do next."

Barquan Blasdel made a hoarse, peculiarly ugly sound: an ejaculation of bitter amusement rendered glottal and

gutteral by hate. His ease and facility of manner had
deserted him; he crouched tensely over the railing of the
rostrum. "Go then to ruined Tranque! All you faithless,
you irreverent ones—get hence and good riddance! Let
Tranque be your home, and let Tranque become a name
accused, an evil odor, a vile disease! Only do not scream
to King Kragen for aid when the rogues, unchided by
the great King, devour your sponges, tear your nets,
crush your coracles!"

"The many cannot be as rapacious as the one," said
Sklar Hast. "Nevertheless, do not be persuaded by the
ranting of the Intercessor. Tranque Float is ruined and
will support but few folk until the nets are repaired and
new arbors seeded. For the present, a migration such as
Blasdel suggests is impractical."

From the red-haired Peculator came a call: "Let the
intercessors take King Kragen and migrate to some far
line of floats; then all of us will be suited!"

Blasdel, making no response, jumped down from the
rostrum and marched off across the float to his private
pad.

Chapter 6

In spite of the strife, or perhaps because it did not seem real, and in spite of the devastation, almost all of the Tranque folk elected to return to their home float. A few, appalled by the circumstances, took up temporary habitation elsewhere, perhaps at the hut of a caste cousin or guild-fellow, but most decided for better or worse to return to Tranque. So they did, silently rowing their coracles, nursing such aches, bruises, or wounds as they had incurred, looking neither left nor right for fear of staring across the water into the face of friend or neighbor whom they had only just desisted from belaboring.

It was a melancholy voyage through the gray-violet evening, down along the line of floats, each with its characteristic silhouette, each with its peculiar ambience or quirk of personality, so that a turn of phrase might be noted as typically Aumerge or a bit of carved wood identified immediately and unmistakably as the work of a Leumar Niggler. And now Tranque, of all the floats, was devastated, Tranque alone. It was enough to make tears of grief and bitterness well from the eyes of the Tranque folk. For them all was changed; the old life would never return. The resentments and bitterness might numb and scar over, but the friendships would never again be easy, the trusts whole. Still, Tranque was home. There was no other place to go.

There was small comfort to be found on Tranque. A third of the huts were in ruins. The granary and all the precious flour had been wasted; the proud tower lay in a tangle of splinters and wreckage. Directly across the float, in a great avenue of destruction, could be traced the course of King Kragen.

On the morning after the convocation the folk stood about in groups, working in a desultory fashion, glancing sidewise in surly silence toward persons whom they had known all their lives. Somewhat to Sklar Hast's surprise Semm Voiderveg had returned to the float, though his own cottage had been crushed by King Kragen and now was only a tangle of crushed withe and tattered padskin. Semm Voiderveg went to look disconsolately at the mess, poking and prodding here and there, extracting an implement, a pot, a bucket, an article of clothing, a volume of Analects sodden from water which had gushed up from a broken place in the float. Feeling Sklar Hast's gaze upon him, he gave an angry shrug and marched away to the undamaged cottage of Arbiter Myrex, with whom he was lodged.

Sklar Hast continued toward his own destination: the hut of the former Master Hoodwink, which also had suffered destruction, though perhaps in lesser degree. Meril Rohan was hard at work, cutting up the rubbish, stacking usable withe and such varnished pad-skin as might feasibly be reused. Sklar Hast silently began to help her, and she made no objection.

At last, protected by a toppled cupboard, she found what she sought: sixty-one folios bound in supple grayfish leather. Sklar Hast carried the volumes to a bench, covered them with a sheet of pad-skin against the possibility of a sudden shower. Meril turned back to the ruined hut, but Sklar Hast took her hand and led her to the bench. She seated herself without argument, and Sklar Hast sat beside her. "I have been anxious to talk to you."

"I expected as much."

Sklar Hast found her composure baffling. What did it signify? Love? Hate? Indifference? Frigidity?

She went on to enlighten him. "I've always had contradicting impulses in regard to you. I admire your energy. Your decisiveness—some call it ruthlessness—makes me uneasy. Your motives are transparent and do you no discredit, although your recklessness and heedlessness do."

Sklar Hast was moved to protest. "I am neither one nor the other! In emergencies one must act without vacillation. Indecisiveness and failure are the same."

Meril nodded toward the ruins. "What do you call this?"

"Not failure. It is a setback, a misfortune, a tragedy—but how could it have been avoided? Assuming, of course, that we intended to free ourselves from King Kragen."

Meril Rohan shrugged. "I don't know the answer. But the decisions which you took alone should have been taken jointly by everyone."

"No," said Sklar Hast stubbornly. "How far would we get, how fast would we be able to react, if at every need for action we were forced to counsel? Think of the outcries and the delay from Myrex and Voiderveg and even your father! Nothing would be accomplished; we would be mired!"

Meril Rohan made restless movements with her hands. Finally she said, "Very well. This is clear. Also it echoes the Memorium of Lester McManus. I forget his exact phrasing, but he remarks that since we are men, and since most of us prefer to be good, we are constantly looking for absolutes. We want no taint on any of our actions, and we can't reconcile ourselves to actions which are in any aspect immoral."

"Unfortunately," said Sklar Hast, "there are very few absolutely moral deeds, except possibly pure passivity—and I am uncertain as to this. It may be there is *no* completely moral act. The more decisive and energetic any act is, the more uncertain will become the chances of its being absolutely moral."

Meril Rohan was amused. "This sounds like a certain 'principle of uncertainty' James Brunet, the scientist, mentions in his Memorium, but which seems quite incomprehensible to me. . . . You may be right—from your point of view. Certainly not from Semm Voiderveg's."

"Nor King Kragen's."

Meril nodded, a faint smile on her lips, and looking at

her, Sklar Hast wondered why he ever had thought to test
other girls of the float when surely this was the one he
wanted. He studied her a moment, trying to decide
wherein lay her charm. Her figure was by no means vol-
uptuous, though it was unmistakably feminine. He had
seen prettier faces, though Meril's face, with its subtle
irregularities and unexpected delicacies of modeling and
quick, almost imperceptible quirks and flexibilities, was
fascination itself.

Now she was pensive and sat looking east across the
water, where the whole line of floats extended, one behind
the other, curving to the north just sufficiently to allow all
to be seen: Thrasneck, Bickle, Sumber, Adelvine, Green
Lamp, Fleurnoy, Aumerge, Quincunx, Fay, all these last
merging into the horizon haze, all the others no more
than lavender-gray smudges on the dark blue ocean.
Above all towered a great billowing white cloud.

Sklar Hast sensed something of her thoughts and drew
a deep breath. "Yes ... It's a beautiful world. If only
there were no King Kragen."

She turned impulsively to him, took his arm. "There are
other floats, to east and west. Why don't we go, leave
King Kragen behind?"

Sklar Hast gloomily shook his head. "King Kragen
wouldn't let us go."

"We could wait until he was at the far west, at Almack
or Sciona, and sail east. He'd never know."

"We could do that—and leave King Kragen supreme.
Do you think this would be the way of the Firsts?"

Meril reflected. "I don't know.... After all, they fled
the tyrants; they did not return to attack them."

"They had no choice! The Ship of Space sank in the
ocean."

Meril shook her head. "They had no intention of attacking anyone. They considered themselves lucky to escape .... Frankly, there is much in the Memoria that
puzzles me, allusions I don't comprehend, especially in
regard to the tyrants."

Sklar Hast picked up Meril's concordance to the Memoria, opened the pages. Spelling out the letters with

difficulty, for his eyes and mind were attuned to hood-wink configurations, he found the entry entitled "Kragen."

Meril, noticing what he read, said, "The references aren't very explicit." She ran her finger swiftly along the references, opened books.

"This is Eleanor Morse: 'All is peace, all is ideal, save only for one rather horrible aquatic beast: fish? insect? echinoderm? The classifications are meaningless, of course. We've decided to call them "kragen."' And Paul van Blee writes: 'About our only spectator sport is watch-ing the kragen and betting which one of us gets eaten first. We've seen some monstrous specimens, up to twenty feet in length. Certainly no encouragement for aquatic sports!' James Brunet, the scientist, says: 'The other day Joe Kamy stuck a tender young kragen, scarcely four feet long, with a sharp stick. Blood—or whatever you wish to call it—ran blue, like some of the terrestrial lobsters and crabs. I wonder if that indicates a similar internal chemistry. Hemoglobin contains iron, chlorophyll, magnesium; hemocyanin, as in blue lobster blood, copper. It's a powerful beast, this kragen, and I'd swear intelligent.' That's about all anyone says about the kragen."

Sklar Hast nodded. "Something that puzzles me and that I can't get away from: if the intercessors are able to communicate with the kragen, even to the extent of summoning it—how do they do it? Through the Master Hoodwink? Does he flash some particular signal? I've never heard of any such system."

"Nor I," said Meril, rather stiffly.

"You can't know," said Sklar Hast, "because you're not a hoodwink."

"I know my father never called King Kragen to Tranque Float."

"Voiderveg admitted that he did so. But how?" He rose to his feet and stood looking off across the float. "Well—I must work with the others." He hesitated a mo-ment, but Meril Rohan offered him no encouragement. "Is there anything you need?" he asked presently. "Re-member, I am Guild-Master now and you are under my protection, so you must call me if there is any lack."

Meril Rohan gave a terse nod.

"Will you be my spouse, untested?" asked Sklar Hast, rather lamely.

"No." Her mood had changed once more, and she had become remote. Sklar Hast wondered why. "I need nothing," she said. "Thank you."

Sklar Hast turned away and went to join those who disassembled the old hoodwink tower. He had acted too precipitously, too awkwardly, he told himself. With Zander Rohan only days dead, Meril undoubtedly still grieved and could hardly be interested in offers of espousal.

He put her from his mind, and joined the hoodwinks and larceners who were salvaging such of the old structure as was useful. Broken withe, fragments of torn pad-skin trash, were taken to a fire-raft floating on the lagoon and burned, and in short order the look of devastation disappeared.

Hooligans meanwhile had raised the net and were repairing the damage. Sklar Hast paused to watch them, then spoke to Roger Kelso, the scrivener, who for reasons of his own had come to Tranque Float. "Imagine a net of heavy hawser hanging over the lagoon. King Kragen swims into the lagoon, anxious to glut himself. The net drops; King Kragen is entangled. . . ." He paused.

"And then?" inquired Roger Kelso with a saturnine grin.

"Then we bind him securely, tow him out to sea and bid him farewell."

Roger Kelso nodded. "Possible—under optimum conditions. I have two objections. First, his mandibles. He might well cut the net in front of him, extend his palps, draw around more of the net, and cut himself free. Secondly, the intercessors. They would observe the suspended net, guess its purpose, and either warn King Kragen away or invite him to come and punish the criminals who sought to kill him."

Sklar Hast sadly agreed. "Whatever means we ultimately fix upon, the intercessors must never learn of it."

The Master Larcener, Rollo Barnack, had heard the conversation. Now he said, "I have also given thought to the problem of King Kragen. A solution has occurred to me: a device of innocent appearance which, if all goes well—and mind you, there is no guarantee of this— but as I say, if all goes precisely, King Kragen might well be killed. Best of all, the vigilance of Semm Voider- veg need not be aroused."

"You interest me extremely," said Sklar Hast. "De- scribe this ingenious device."

Rollo Barnack started to speak, but, noting the ap- proach of Arbiter Ixon Myrex, Intercessor Semm Voider- veg, and several others of like conviction, held his tongue.

Arbiter Myrex was spokesman for the group. His voice was clear, firm, and unemotional; clearly the confronta- tion had been discussed and rehearsed. "Sklar Hast, we speak to you now in a spirit not necessarily of amity, but at least one of compromise."

Sklar Hast nodded warily. "Speak on."

"You will agree that chaos, disorder, destruction, and contention must be halted, absolutely and definitely; that Tranque Float must be restored to its former high status and reputation." He looked at Sklar Hast expectantly.

"Continue," said Sklar Hast.

"You make no response," complained Ixon Myrex.

"You asked no question," said Sklar Hast. "You merely uttered an asseveration."

Ixon Myrex made a petulant gesture. "Do you so agree?"

"Certainly," said Sklar Hast. "Do you expect me to argue otherwise?"

Arbiter Myrex ignored the question. "We must neces- sarily cooperate. It is impossible that conditions can re- turn to normal unless all of us exert ourselves to this end, and—er—make certain sacrifices." He paused, but Sklar Hast made no remark. "Essentially, it seems ab- surd and paradoxical that you, with your fanatically un- orthodox views, should continue in an office which carries great weight and prestige. The best interests of the float are served by your voluntary relinquishment of the office."

"Indeed. And what sacrifices do you propose to make?"

"We are agreed that if you display a sense of responsibility, relinquish the guild-mastership, make a sober, sincere profession of orthodoxy, we will remit your delinquencies and hold them no longer to your discredit."

"This is magnanimity indeed," sneered Sklar Hast. "What sort of blubbering water-sheep do you take me for?"

Ixon Myrex nodded curtly. "We feared that this might be your response. Now violence is as abhorrent to us as it is to every man and woman of the floats, and therefore we make no threats. Nevertheless we require from you a solemn undertaking never again to engage in unorthodox activities, or those which challenge the authority of King Kragen."

"And if I don't?"

"Then we will ask that you depart Tranque Float."

"And where do you suggest that I go?"

Semm Voiderveg could contain his passion no longer. He pointed a white quivering finger to the sea. "We suggest that you and others of your ilk depart! There are other floats; they are mentioned in the Analects; the Firsts saw them when the Ship of Space came down. Go forth then to some other float and allow us who wish peace to live as we always have."

Sklar Hast's lip curled. "What of King Kragen? It seems that you contravene the Covenant, suggesting that I trespass upon his ocean. What of that?"

"The trespass then becomes an issue between you and King Kragen! The affair is none of mine."

"And if King Kragen follows us to our new domicile, deserting the Home Floats? What would the intercessors do then?"

Semm Voiderveg blinked. The concept clearly took him by surprise. "If such an exigency arises, be assured that we will know how to deal with it."

Sklar Hast prepared to return to his work. "I will not resign my rightful guild-mastership; I promise no fidelity to you or King Kragen; I will not set forth across the ocean."

Semm Voiderveg started to speak, but Ixon Myrex

held up his hand. "What then do you plan?" he asked
cannily.

Sklar Hast stared at him a long moment, with conflict-
ing impulses struggling inside his brain. All prudence
and sagacity urged him to dissemble, to feign orthodoxy or at least disinterest, while he arrived at some
method to kill King Kragen. But what if he failed in
the attempt? Then once again Tranque Float would
be devastated and people who wanted nothing to do
with the project would be injured, even killed. It seemed
only just that he announce his intentions, in order to give
those who disapproved a chance to remove themselves.

But by so warning Ixon Myrex and Semm Voiderveg
he guaranteed himself of their vigilance, their antagonism, and possibly their interference. It was simple
common sense and good generalship to dissemble, to calm
Ixon Myrex and Semm Voiderveg and blunt their
suspicions. What if a few innocent persons did get
killed? No battles were won without casualties. And Sklar
Hast tried to twist his tongue to speak evasion and re-
assurance, but he could not do it; he was physically unable to put on the necessary mask, and felt a great anger for his own weakness.

"If I were you," he said roughly, "I'd depart Tranque
Float and stay away. Because there might well be further unorthodoxy, as you call it."

"Exactly in what degree?" asked Ixon Myrex crisply.

"I've made no plans. I wouldn't tell you in any event.
But now, against my better judgment, I've warned you."

Semm Voiderveg once more began to speak, but once
more Ixon Myrex silenced him. "I see that our attempt
at a harmonious solution is in vain. You warned me; I
will warn you. Any attempt to offend King Kragen, any
attempt upon his dignity will be regarded as a capital
crime. That is my judgment as Arbiter of Tranque
Float! You have challenged authority and the majesty
of tradition. Beware that your impudence does not bring
you to grief!"

One of the others spoke: Gian Recargo, the Bezzler Elder, a man of great gentility, rectitude, and presence.

"Sklar Hast, are you aware of your irresponsibility? You threaten the lives and properties of others who wish no part of your mad antics; do you not feel shame?"

"I have thought at length about the situation," said Sklar Hast. "I have concluded that a great evil exists, that inertia and fear press so heavily upon otherwise worthy folk like yourself that you abide this evil. Someone must be willing to take great risks, even with the lives of other people. This is not irresponsibility; it is far more responsibility than I relish. The judgment is not solely my own; I am no monomaniac. Many other sane and responsible folk agree with me that King Kragen must be defeated. Why do you not join us? Once the sea-beast is destroyed, we are free. Is not this worth the risk? We can use the ocean as we please! We need feed the gluttonous maw no longer! The intercessors will be deprived of their sinecures and must then work like the rest of us, which appalls them; hence their antagonism. This is the way the future must go!"

Gian Recargo was silent. Ixon Myrex tugged irritably on his beard. A heavy half moment went by. Semm Voiderveg looked at them impatiently. "Why do you not refute this incredible diatribe?"

Gian Recargo turned away to look out over the lagoon. "I must think at length," he muttered. "I do not care to hear such a challenge to my courage."

"Bah," said Ixon Myrex uneasily. "Conditions were well enough in the past. Who wants to sail the ocean? And the sponges consumed by King Kragen are not a staggering tax upon us."

Semm Voiderveg smote the air with his fist. "This is superficial! The issue is Sklar Hast's abominable arrogance, his disrespect and irreverence toward our great King Kragen!"

Gian Recargo turned on his heel and walked slowly off across the float. Semm Voiderveg made another angry gesticulation. Ixon Myrex held his ground a moment longer, turned a searching gaze upon ruined tower, lagoon, Sklar Hast, the others who stood attentively about, then made a nondescript sound and marched away.

The hoodwinks and larceners returned to work. Sklar Hast, with Roger Kelso, went off to confer with Rollo Barnack, to hear his plan for killing King Kragen. Both agreed that if conditions were right, if timing were precise, if the materials were sufficiently tough, King Kragen might well be killed.

Chapter 7

Gradually the evidence of disaster disappeared; gradually Tranque Float resumed its normal aspect. The broken huts and shattered timbers were burned on the fire-raft, and the ashes carefully stored for later use in the manufacture of soap, whitewash, fire-brick, the mordanting of cloth, the weighting of sinkers, the clarification of varnish. The corpses, after two weeks' submersion in special receptacles, during which time certain small finned worms stripped the flesh from the bones, were conveyed to a remote part of the float where the hardest bones were removed, and the remainder calcined for lime: a work which traditionally had been the exclusive domain of advertisermen.

Withe had been cut, seasoned, formed into new huts, covered with pad-skin and varnished; new sponge arbors had been built, seeded with floss and lowered into the bright blue water.

The hoodwink tower, the most massive and complicated object of the float, was the last structure to be rebuilt. The new tower was even taller than the old, more massive in design, with a site somewhat closer to the lagoon.

The method of construction was also different from the old and elicited considerable comment among the folk of Tranque Float. Customarily each leg descended through a hole in the float to be anchored in the crotch of a sturdy underwater stem. In the new tower these supports terminated in a low platform twenty-five feet square, and from this platform rose the four legs: great poles a hundred feet long fabricated from lengths of withe laid in varnish and whipped. The legs, held rigid by spreaders, gradually converged, to terminate in a frame six feet square.

The proportions of the tower, the mass of the poles, and the comparatively small area of the base platform, aroused as much curiosity and criticism as the unconventional method of construction. Ixon Myrex on one occasion taxed Rollo Barnack, the Master Larcener, with unorthodoxy.

"Never have I seen a tower of this sort before!" he complained. "I see no need for such heavy construction. The posts are as staunch above as they are below: why is this?"

"It lends an added solidity," declared Rollo Barnack with a wise wink.

"Solid perhaps, but so precariously narrow at the base that a good gust of wind will tip it over and hurl it into the lagoon!"

"Do you really think so?" Rollo Barnack asked earnestly, standing back and inspecting the tower as if this were his first clear view of it.

"I am no larcener," Ixon Myrex went on, "and I know little enough of construction, but this is how it appears to me. Especially when the tower house is built aloft and the lamps and hoods hung on the cross-arm! Think of the force, the leverage!"

"You are quite right," said Rollo Barnack. "To counteract this force we propose to run guy-lines."

The Arbiter shook his head in puzzlement. "Why did you not build in the old manner, with legs sufficiently outspread so that the guy-lines were not needed? This seems overcomplicated to me."

"We use much less float area," Rollo Barnack pointed out. "This is a significant consideration."

Ixon Myrex shook his head without conviction, but made no further protest.

So the guy-lines were extended. Next the control house was added, then the great yardarm on which the hoods and lamps hung. This last was constructed with the most meticulous care, from sections of the densest stem obtainable. Ixon Myrex, once again inspecting the construction, was astounded by the mass of the yardarm. In explanation, Rollo Barnack referred to the consequent lack of vibration and the greater control thus afforded the hoodwinks. "Have no fear, Arbiter. Every detail in the construction of this tower has been carefully thought out."

"Like the guy-ropes, I suppose?" Ixon Myrex inquired sarcastically. "And the manner in which the legs are affixed to the base platform—bound, no less! By ropes! Is this a solid manner in which to build a hoodwink tower?"

"We hope it will fulfill its purpose," Rollo Barnack said. "If it does this, we shall ask no more of it."

And again Ixon Myrex departed, shaking his head.

During this time King Kragen had not appeared in the vicinity of Tranque Float.

From the Thrasneck hoodwink tower came occasional news of his whereabouts: He had been seen cruising to the south of Sankston heading west; he had put in at Populous Equity to feed; he had fed again at Parnassus, the float next west. Thereafter he submerged, and for two days nothing was heard of him.

Tranque was almost back to normal. The sponges were growing large and beginning to burst from their husks; the huts had all been rebuilt; the new hoodwink tower, if somewhat ponderous and top-heavy, stood tall and impressive.

The yardarm had been a long time in preparation. Each end was tapered to a point and boiled in varnish for three days, then baked over a slow fire, until the stem was hard and dense. Along the lengths were fixed reinforcing struts, and all scraped and buffed and oiled so it shone smooth and glossy.

Finally the yardarm was hoisted to the top of the tower and secured in place, and again no precaution seemed too great. First it was seated in a socket, then glued, lashed, and pegged.

Once more Ixon Myrex was baffled. "The tower stands askew!"

"How so?" asked Rollo Barnack mildly.

"Notice how it fronts—not directly upon the Thrasneck Tower as it should, but considerably to the side. The folk on Thrasneck will read all our winks with a squint, sidelong."

Rollod Barnack nodded judiciously. "We are not unaware of this condition. It was planned in this manner, for the following reasons. First, it is rumored that the Thrasneck folk are planning a new tower, to be constructed somewhere along the line in which we now face. Second, the configuration of the underwater stems has made it difficult to fix the posts at any other angle than as you see, and we believe that in time there will be a gradual turning and twisting, which will bring the tower more directly to bear upon the current Thrasneck tower."

Intercessor Semm Voiderveg, who had regained something of his former poise, joined Ixon Myrex's criticisms.

"This seems the least graceful and efficient tower I have ever seen! Notice that long, heavy, pointed yardarm, and that narrow, elongated cabin below. Has anyone ever seen the like before?"

Rollo Barnack repeated his former remark. "It looks more than efficient to me. If it fulfills its purpose, we will be more than happy."

Ixon Myrex shook his head sadly. "The folk of other floats believe us eccentric and perverse as it is; with this new tower staring blankly to sea, they will consider us lunatics."

"Correctly, perhaps," said Sklar Hast with a grin. "Why don't you and Voiderveg depart?"

"Let us not talk about matters of the past!" muttered Ixon Myrex. "It all seems a bad dream, as if it never happened."

"Unfortunately it did," said Sklar Hast, "and King Kragen still swims the sea. If only he would die of natural causes, or choke on a surfeit of sponges, or drown!"

Semm Voiderveg studied him levelly. "You are a man without reverence, without fidelity."

Ixon Myrex and Semm Voiderveg presently departed. Sklar Hast watched them go. "What a situation!" he complained to Roger Kelso. "We cannot act like honorable men; we cannot declare ourselves; instead we must skulk about in this half-brazen, half-furtive pretense."

"It is pointless to worry about the matter," said Kelso. "The choice long since was made; we are now ready to act."

"And if we fail?"

Roger Kelso shrugged. "I put our chances of success as one in three. All must go with such exactness, such precision of timing as to make optimism out of the question."

Sklar Hast said, "We must warn the folk of the float. This is the very least we can do."

Rollo Barnack and Roger Kelso argued but without success. Sklar Hast finally had his way, and in the early part of the evening he called a meeting of all the folk of the float.

He spoke briefly and to the point. "Tranque Float is once more whole. Life seems to be placid and even. It is only fair to announce that this is illusory. Many of us are not reconciled to the overlordship of King Kragen, and we propose to end it. We may be unsuccessful; there may be a new and even more disastrous set of circumstances in the future. So all are warned, and are welcome to leave Tranque for other more orthodox floats."

Ixon Myrex jumped to his feet. "Sklar Hast—you may not involve the rest of us in your scheme! It is not right! This is my judgment as Arbiter."

Sklar Hast made no response.

Semm Voiderveg spoke. "Naturally I endorse the Arbiter's views! And may I ask how you propose to implement your preposterous schemes?"

"We are evolving a strain of poisonous sponges," Roger

Kelso told him. "When King Kragen eats, he will become waterlogged and sink."

Sklar Hast turned away, walked to the edge of the float to look off across the water. Behind him was further wrangling; then by twos and threes and fours, the folk went off to their various huts.

Meril Rohan came to join Sklar Hast, and for a moment both looked off across the twilight. Meril Rohan said, "This is a difficult time we live in, without clearcut rights and wrongs, and it is hard to know how to act."

"An era has come to an end," said Sklar Hast. "A Golden Age, an Age of Innocence—it is ended. Violence, hate, turbulence have come to the floats. The world will never be the same again."

"A new and better world may come of it all."

Sklar Hast shook his head. "I doubt it. If King Kragen foundered and sank at this moment, there would still be changes. It seems as if suddenly the time were ripe for change. We must go forward—or go back."

Meril Rohan was silent. Then she pointed toward Thrasneck. "Watch the winks."

". . . King . . . Kragen . . . seen . . . to . . . the . . . north . . . of . . . Quincunx . . . proceeding . . . in . . . an . . . easterly . . . direction. . . ."

"The time is not yet," said Sklar Hast. "We are not quite ready."

The next day King Kragen was seen to the north of Tranque Float, drifting idly without apparent purpose. For an hour he floated placidly, eye-tubes fixed on Tranque, then veered close as if in curiosity, and gave Tranque a brief inspection. Semm Voiderveg, arrayed in his ceremonial robes, came forth to stand at the edge of the float, where he performed his ritual postures and beckonings. King Kragen watched a moment or two, then, reacting to some unknowable emotion, gave a quick jerk and with a surge of his vanes swung about and swam to the west, mandibles scissoring, palps pushing in and out.

Semm Voiderveg made a final genuflection, and watched King Kragen's departure.

Nearby stood Sklar Hast, and as Semm Voiderveg

turned to go back to his hut, his gaze met that of Sklar
Hast. For a brief moment the two men studied each other,
with a hostility in which there existed no understanding.
Sklar Hast felt an emotion far different from the simple
contempt he felt for Ixon Myrex. It was as if Semm
Voiderveg were himself part kragen, as if in his veins
flowed a thick indigo ooze instead of red human blood.

A week later King Kragen feasted on Bickle sponges,
and the next day did likewise at Thrasneck. On the day
following, a hundred yards from the entrance to Tranque
lagoon, he slowly surfaced and once more gave Tranque
Float a deliberate, almost suspicious scrutiny.

As Semm Voiderveg ran forth in his ceremonial
robes, Sklar Hast mounted the ladder to the hoodwink
house, but King Kragen slowly submerged. The water
swirled over his domed black turret; the sea lay calm
and blue as before.

Sklar Hast came down from the tower to meet Semm
Voiderveg returning to his hut. "King Kragen is vigilant! He knows Tranque Float for the haunt of evil that
it is! Beware!" And Semm Voiderveg strode off in a flut-
ter of black.

Sklar Hast looked after him, wondering if Semm Voiderveg were perhaps mad. Returning to the open-sided
shed, where with a number of apprentices and assistant
hoodwinks he was constructing a pair of what he referred to as "practice mechanisms," he discussed the
possibility with Ben Kell, the Assistant Master Hoodwink, who had no opinion.

"In Voiderveg's opinion you are mad," said Kell.
"These are difficult matters to define. In the context of
a year ago, Voiderveg is saner than sane. With conditions as they are now, the question of who is most sane
wavers on an edge."

Sklar Hast grinned sourly. He had lost weight; his
cheeks had become a trifle concave, and there was a
sprinkle of gray in the hair at his temples. "Let's take
these things outside and give Myrex something new to
worry over."

The mechanisms were carried out and set on the float halfway between the tower and the lagoon, one to the right, one to the left. In the lagoon, broad on the tower, hung a large arbor already ripe with sponges. Twenty feet beyond, apparently by sheer chance, floated a chip of wood. The chip, the two practice mechanisms, and the tower formed a rough square seventy feet on a side.

Stakes were driven into the substance of the float; the mechanisms were anchored firmly. Upon each was a sighting device, similar to a navigator's pelorus, which Sklar Hast adjusted to bear on the floating chip.

He had prophesied correctly. Almost immediately the Arbiter appeared with his now familiar doubts and criticisms. He began in a tone of weary patience, "What are these objects?"

"These are practice machines for the apprentices. We will leave them here until suitable accommodation is arranged under the tower."

"Seemingly you would equip the tower with frames, hoods, and lamps before constructing practice machines."

"Normally we would do so. But we are testing a new linkage, and it would not be well to allow the apprentices to scamp their practice."

"In the meantime we can send no messages. We are isolated."

Sklar Hast pointed to the Thrasneck tower. "You can read all that transpires elsewhere. Nothing of consequence occurs here."

"Nevertheless, we should put our system into working order as rapidly as possible." And he gave the tower a black look. "Awkward, top-heavy, and askew as it is."

"If it achieves its purpose," said Sklar Hast, "it will be the most beautiful object the world has yet seen."

Arbiter Myrex gave him a sharp glance. "What is the meaning of that remark?"

Sklar Hast saw that he had gone too far. Ixon Myrex was a slow and rigid man, but not stupid. "Sheer exuberance, sheer hyperbole."

Ixon Myrex grunted. "The structure is an aesthetic disgrace. Already we are the laughingstock of the whole

line. When the folk speak of Quatrefoil and Sankston
for extravagance and eccentricity, now they will add
Tranque. I would not be sorry to see it destroyed and
another erected in its place."

"This one will serve," said Sklar Hast carelessly.

Further days passed. King Kragen dined at Green Lamp,
at Fleurnoy, and at Adelvine three days running, then
swam far west to Granolt. For two days he was seen no
more, then appeared far out on the horizon to the south
of Aumerge, coasting east. The following day he dined
once more at Adelvine, to the near depletion of the
Adelvine lagoon, and the following day at Sumber, the
third float north from Tranque, with only Thrasneck
and Bickle between. On Tranque Float a mood of uneasiness and foreboding manifested itself. People spoke
in hushed voices and looked constantly sidelong toward
the sea. By some sort of psychic osmosis all knew that
a great project was afoot, even though the nature of the
project was unknown—to all but about thirty or so of the
most secretive men of the float.

Two days after King Kragen dined at Sumber, he appeared in the ocean to the north of Tranque and lay
floating for half an hour, twitching his great vanes. At
this, certain of the more timorous departed Tranque, conveying themselves, their women and children to Thrasneck.

Semm Voiderveg stormed up to Sklar Hast. "What is
going on? What do you plan?"

"More to the point," said Sklar Hast, "what do you
plan?"

"What do I plan?" bellowed the portly Intercessor,
"What else do I plan but rectitude? It is you and your accomplices who threaten the fabric of our existence!"

"Calm yourself, Voiderveg," said Wall Bunce with an
insensitive grin. "Yonder floats the kragen to which you
have pledged yourself. If you appear at a disadvantage,
you forfeit his respect."

Rudolf Snyder gave a cry of warning. "He moves! He
swims forward!"

Semm Voiderveg made a wild gesture. "I must go to

welcome him. Sklar Hast, I warn you, I implore you, do
nothing contrary to the Covenant!"

Sklar Hast made no reply. With a final desperate glare
of admonition, the Intercessor marched to the edge of
the float and began his ritual gesticulations.

King Kragen moved slowly forward, by small twitches
and flicks of the vanes. The eye-tubes studied the float
carefully, as if something of the tension and emotion of
those on the float had reached him.

King Kragen approached the mouth of the lagoon. Semm
Voiderveg signaled his assistants, who drew back the
net to allow King Kragen access into the lagoon.

The great black bulk approached. Sklar Hast became
conscious of the close attention of Ixon Myrex and several
others. It was clear that counsel had been taken and plans
made to forestall any action on his part. Sklar Hast had
expected something of the sort and was not perturbed.
He went to a bench and seated himself, as if contemptuously disassociating himself from the entire affair. Looking around, he saw that others of orthodox persuasion
similarly stood near Roger Kelso and Rubal Gallager,
apparently ready to employ forcible restraint, if the
necessity arose. Elsewhere about the float, others of the
conspiracy were casually going to their places. To Sklar
Hast it seemed that the program was blatantly obvious,
and he wondered that neither Semm Voiderveg, Ixon Myrex, nor any of those who supported them had perceived
it.

There was one who had: Gian Recargo, Elder of the
Bezzlers. He came now to the bench and seated himself
beside Sklar Hast. "This is a precarious hour." He glanced
up toward the hoodwink tower. "I hope, for all our sakes,
that all goes well."

Sklar Hast nodded grimly. "So do I."

Time moved with nerve-racking slowness. The sun
shone almost perpendicularly upon the ultramarine water. The foliage—black, orange, green, purple, tawny yellow—swayed in the faintest of warm breezes. Into the lagoon swam King Kragen. Semm Voiderveg ran to the

edge of the float and performed his gestures of reverence and invitation.

Sklar Hast frowned, rubbed his chin. Gian Recargo glanced at him sidewise. "What of Semm Voiderveg?" he asked in the driest of voices.

"I had not considered him," muttered Sklar Hast. "A flaw in my thinking . . . I will do my best for him." He rose to his feet, joined Rollo Barnack who lounged beside one of the practice mechanisms. At the other one stood Ben Kell, the Assistant Master Hoodwink, both in a position where they could sight across their peloruses. "The Intercessor stands in the way," Sklar Hast muttered. "Pay him no heed. I will try to save him."

"It will be dangerous for you as well."

Sklar Hast nodded. "Unfortunately this is so. All of us are running grave risks. Heed neither Semm Voiderveg nor myself. Proceed as if neither of us were imperiled. We will both escape."

Rollo Barnack nodded. "As you wish." And he looked across the pelorus, to see a twitching tip of King Kragen's forward vane.

King Kragen floated quietly ten or twenty seconds, studying Semm Voiderveg. Once again he eased forward, thrust forth his palps, and gave himself a last thrust which pushed him close to the arbor.

King Kragen began to feed.

Rollo Barnack, looking along the points of his pelorus, found the turret slightly to the right of his line of sight. He waited. King Kragen floated a trifle to the left. Rollo Barnack gave a prearranged signal, raising his hand, running his fingers through his hair. Ben Kell, at the other pelorus, was already doing likewise.

At the back of the tower Poe Belrod and Wall Bunce already had cut the bindings that lashed the two rear legs to the stubs rising from the base platform. Rudolf Snyder and Garth Gasselton loosed the rear guy-lines. At each of the fore guy-lines—those leading toward the lagoon—five men pulled as casually and nonchalantly as possible.

The great tower, tall, heavy, narrow-based, pivoted

over on the two legs yet bound. The great pointed yardarm began to sweep out a great arc that would terminate upon King Kragen's turret.

Directly in the path of the falling tower stood Semm
Voiderveg, intent at his rituals. Sklar Hast strode forward to thrust the Intercessor out of the way. Others
realized that the tower was falling. There came sudden startled screams. Semm Voiderveg looked over his shoulder
to see the toppling structure and likewise sensed Sklar
Hast lunging at him. He gave a strangled croak, and,
trying to run, stumbled with flapping arms. Both men
rolled clear. The astounded King Kragen gave a twitch
of the vanes. Down like an enormous pickax came the
tower, and the pointed yardarm missed the turret dead
center only by the amount of King Kragen's twitch of
alarm. Down upon the black barrel came the point,
glancing away and burying itself in the black rectangular
pad below.

From Rollo Barnack and Roger Kelso came groans of
disappointment; others screamed in horror and fright.
King Kragen himself emitted a fierce, whistling hiss
and thrashed out with all four vanes. The yardarm
snapped from the tower; King Kragen surged struggling
back into the lagoon. With two of the palps it seized the
stump still protruding from its flesh, snatched it forth
and brandished it high in the air. Semm Voiderveg, struggling to his feet, called out in a shrill, sobbing voice,
"Mercy, King Kragen, a terrible mistake! Mercy, have
mercy!"

King Kragen surged close and brought the length of
timber vindictively down on Semm Voiderveg, crushing
him to the pad. Again he struck, then roaring and
hissing hurled the object at Sklar Hast. Then, backing
up and accelerating forward, he charged the float.

"Run," cried Rollo Barnack hoarsely. "Run for your
lives!"

King Kragen was not content with the devastation
of Tranque. He likewise wrought havoc upon Thrasneck
and Bickle; then, fatigued or perhaps in pain, he propelled himself to sea and disappeared.

Chapter 8

A Grand Convocation was called on Apprise Float. Barquan Blasdel, the Apprise Intercessor, was the first to speak. His remarks were predictably bitter, his manner grim. He eulogized Semm Voiderveg at length; he lamented the dead of Tranque, Thrasneck, and Bickle; he described the havoc and disaster; he speculated pessimistically regarding the status of the broken Covenant. "His comprehensible fury is not yet assuaged, but do the guilty suffer? No. This morning King Kragen attacked and demolished the coracles of four Vidmar swindlers. Who can blame him? To come in good faith, under the terms of the Covenant, to receive his just due, encouraged and welcomed by the Intercessor—and then to experience this murderous attack! King Kragen has demonstrated restraint in not destroying every float of the chain!

"Needless to say, the wretched conspirators who hatched this plot must be punished. The last convocation ended in riot and bloodshed. We must be more controlled, more sagacious on this occasion, but we must definitely act. The conspirators must die."

Barquan Blasdel did not call for a show of fists, since the accused had not yet spoken in their behalf.

Phyral Berwick, the Apprise Arbiter, hence convocation moderator, looked around the float. "Who cares to speak?"

"I." Gian Recargo, Elder of the Tranque Bezzlers, came forward. "I was not an active conspirator. Initially I was of the orthodox view; then I changed my thinking. It

97

is still changed. The so-called conspirators indeed have brought damage and loss of life to the floats. They grieve for this as much as anyone else. But the damage and the deaths are inevitable, because I have come to agree with Sklar Hast. King Kragen must be killed. So let us not revile these men who by dint of great ingenuity and daring almost killed King Kragen. They did as well as they were able to. Sklar Hast risked his own life to save the life of Semm Voiderveg. King Kragen killed the Intercessor."

Barquan Blasdel leaped to his feet and ridiculed Gian Recargo's defense of what he called the "blasphemous irresponsibility of the conspirators." After him spoke Archibel Verack, Quincunx Intercessor; then Parensic Mole, the Wyebolt Arbiter; then in succession other arbiters, intercessors, elders and guild-masters.

There was clearly no consensus. It seemed as if approximately a third of those present favored the most drastic penalties for the conspirators; another third, while regretting the destruction and death toll, regretted even more strongly the failure of the plot; while the final third were persons confused, indecisive, and fearful, who swayed first in one direction, then another.

Sklar Hast, advised by Gian Recargo, did not speak, and only watched and listened stonily as Barquan Blasdel and others heaped opprobrium upon him.

The afternoon drew on, and tempers began to grow short. Barquan Blasdel finally decided to bring matters to a head. In a voice deadly calm he again enumerated the sins of Sklar Hast and his fellows, then pitching his voice at a compelling level, called for a show of fists. "Peace and the Covenant! All who favor this, raise their fists! We must purge the evil that threatens us! And I say"—he leaned forward, looked menacingly across the float—"that if the convocation does not correctly vote death to the murderers, we right-thinkers and true-believers must organize ourselves into a disciplined group, to make sure that justice is done! The matter is this serious, this basic, this important! Crime may not go unpunished! We vacillated before—see where it took us! So I say to you, vote death to the murderers, or see justice sternly imposed by the mighty force of orthodox anger. So now: Fists high against Sklar Hast and the conspirators!"

Fists thrust into the air. An equal number stayed down, though many of these belonged to the confused and un-decided. Now began the ominous mutter of argument that had preceded the bloodshed at the last convocation.

Sklar Hast jumped to his feet, strode to the rostrum. "Clearly we are divided. Some wish to serve King Kra-gen, others prefer not to do so. We are on the verge of a terrible experience, which by all means must be pre-vented. There is one simple way to do this. Other floats as fertile as these exist. I propose to depart these beloved Home Floats and make a new life elsewhere. I naturally will welcome all who wish to join me, though I urge this course upon no one. We will gain freedom. We will serve no King Kragen. Our life will be our own. Undoubtedly there will be initial deprivations, but we shall overcome them and build a life as pleasant as that of Home—per-haps more pleasant because there will be no tyrannical King Kragen. Who then wishes to sail away to a new home?"

A few hands raised, then others, and others still, to represent perhaps a third of those present.

"This is more than I expected," said Sklar Hast. "Go then to your floats, load your coracles with tools, pots, varnish, cordage—all your utile goods. Then return here, to Apprise Lagoon. We will await a propitious time to depart, when the sea-beast is known to be at Sciona, should we choose to sail east, or at Tranque, should we sail west. Needless to say, the direction and hour of de-parture must remain secret. There is no reason to explain why." He cast an ironic glance toward Barquan Blasdel, who sat like a carved image. "It is a sad thing to leave an ancestral home, but it is worse to remain and submit to tyranny. The Firsts made this same decision, and it is clear that at least some of us still retain the ideals of our forefathers."

Barquan Blasdel spoke without rising to his feet: a

crass act. "Don't talk of ideals—merely go. Go gladly.
Go with all goodwill. We will not miss you. And never
seek to return when the teeming rogues, unchided by the
great king, devour your poor sponges, tear your nets,
crush your coracles!"

Sklar Hast ignored him. "All then who will depart these
sad Home Floats, we meet here in two days' time. We
will then secretly decide our hour of departure."

Barquan Blasdel laughed. "You need not fear our interference. Depart whenever you desire; indeed we will
facilitate your going."

Sklar Hast reflected a moment. "You will not inform
King Kragen of our going?"

"No. Of course, he may learn of the fact through his
own observation."

"This will be our plan then. On the evening of the third
day, when the wind blows fair to the west, we depart—
provided, of course, that King Kragen cruises to the east."

Chapter 9

Barquan Blasdel the Apprise Intercessor, his spouse
and six daughters occupied a pad on the ocean to the
north of the main Apprise float, somewhat isolated and
apart. It was perhaps the choicest and most pleasant
pad of the Apprise complex, situated where Blasdel could
read the hoodwink towers of Apprise, of Quatrefoil and
The Bandings to the east, of Granolt to the west. The pad
was delightfully overgrown with a hundred different
plants and vines, some yielding resinous pods, others
capsules of fragrant sap; others crisp tendrils and shoots.
Certain shrubs produced stains and pigment; a purple-
leaved epiphyte yielded a rich-flavored pith. Other growths
were entirely ornamental—a situation not too usual along
the floats, where space was at a premium and every
growing object weighed for its utility. Along the entire
line of floats few pads could compare to that of Barquan
Blasdel for beauty, variety of plantings, isolation, and
calm.

In late afternoon of the second day after the convocation, Barquan Blasdel returned to his pad. He dropped the
painter of his coracle over a stake of carved bone, gazed
appreciatively into the west. The sun had just departed
the sky, which now glowed with effulgent greens, blues,
and, at the zenith, a purple of exquisite purity. The
ocean, rippling to the first whispers of the evening breeze,
reflected the sky. Blasdel felt surrounded, immersed in
color. . . .

He turned away, marched to his house, whistling be-

101

tween his teeth. In the lagoon were five hundred coracles, perhaps as many as six hundred, loaded with goods: the property of the most perverse and troublesome elements of the floats. On the morrow they would depart, and no more would be heard from them. Ever again. And Blasdel's whistling became slow and thoughtful.

Although life seemingly flowed smoothly, he had sensed recently the awakening of an uneasiness, a dissatisfaction, which had made itself felt in a hundred different ways. Barquan Blasdel had not been quite so surprised by the attempt upon King Kragen's life as he professed to be, though for a fact the attempt had approached success more nearly than he would have expected. A clever, unscrupulous fellow, that Sklar Hast. An obstreperous, recalcitrant, skeptical man of great energy, whom Barquan Blasdel was more than happy to have out of the way.

All was working out for the best. Indeed, indeed, indeed! The affair could not have resolved itself more smoothly if he had personally arranged the entire sequence of events! At one stroke all the grumblers, ne'er-do-wells, the covertly insolent, the obstinate hardheads—at one stroke all would disappear, never again to trouble the easy and orthodox way of life!

Almost jauntily Barquan Blasdel ambled up the path to his residence: a group of five semidetached huts, screened by the garden from the main float, and so providing a maximum of privacy for Blasdel, his spouse, and six daughters. Blasdel halted. On a bench beside the door sat a man. Twilight murk concealed his face. Blasdel frowned, peered. Intruders upon his private pad were not welcome.

Blasdel marched forward. The man rose from the bench and bowed; it was Phyral Berwick, the Apprise Arbiter. "Good evening," said Berwick. "I trust I did not startle you."

"By no means," said Blasdel shortly. With rank equal to his own, Berwick could not be ignored, although after his extraordinary and equivocal conduct at the two convocations, Blasdel could not bring himself to display more than a minimum of formal courtesy. He said, "Unfortunately I was not expecting callers and can offer you no refreshment."

"A circumstance of no moment," declared Berwick. "I desire neither food nor drink." He waved his hand around the pad. "You live on a pad of surpassing beauty, Barquan Blasdel. Many envy you."

Blasdel shrugged. "My conduct is orthodox; I am armored against adverse opinion. But what urgency brings you here? I fear that I must be less than ceremonious; I am shortly due at the hoodwink tower to participate in a coded all-float conference."

Berwick made a gesture of polite acquiescence. "My business is of small moment. But I would not keep you standing out here in the dusk. Shall we enter?"

Blasdel grunted, opened the door, allowed Berwick to pass into the hut. From a cupboard he brought luminant fiber, which he set aglow and arranged in a holder. Turning a quick side glance toward Berwick, he said, "In all candor, I am somewhat surprised to see you. Apparently you were among the most vehement of those dissidents who planned to depart."

"I may well have given that impression," Berwick agreed. "But you must realize that declarations uttered in the heat of emotion are occasionally amended in the light of sober reason."

Blasdel nodded curtly. "True enough. I suspect that many other of the ingrates will think twice before joining this harebrained expedition." Though he hoped not.

"This is partly the reason for my presence here," said Berwick. He looked around the room. "An interesting chamber. You own dozens of valuable artifacts. Where are the others of your family?"

"In the domestic area. This is my sanctum, my workroom, my place of meditation."

"Indeed." Berwick inspected the walls. "Indeed, indeed! I believe I notice certain relics of the forefathers!"

"True," said Blasdel. "This small flat object is of the substance called 'metal,' and is extremely hard. The best bone knife will not scratch it. The purpose of this particu-

lar object I cannot conjecture. It is an heirloom. These
books are exact copies of the Memoria. Alas! I find much
in them beyond my comprehension. There is nothing more
of any great interest. On the shelf—my ceremonial head-
dresses; you have seen them before. Here is my telescope. It is old; the case is warped, the gum of the lenses
has bulged and cracked. It was poor gum, to begin with,
but I have little need for a better instrument. My posses-
sions are few. Unlike many intercessors and certain
arbiters"—here he cast a meaningful eye at Phyral Berwick—"I do not choose to surround myself with sybaritic
cushions and baskets of sweetmeats."

Berwick laughed ruefully. "You have touched upon my
weaknesses. Perhaps the fear of deprivation has occa-
sioned second thoughts in me."

"Ha, ha!" Blasdel became jovial. "I begin to understand. The scalawags who set off to wild new floats can
expect nothing but hardship: wild fish, horny sponges,
new varnish with little more body than water; in short
they will be returning to the life of savages. They must
expect to suffer the depredations of lesser kragen, who
will swiftly gather. Perhaps in time . . ." His voice
dwindled; his face took on a thoughtful look.

"You were about to say?" prompted Phyral Berwick.

Blasdel gave a noncommittal laugh. "An amusing, if
farfetched conceit crossed my mind. Perhaps in time
one of these lesser kragen will vanquish the others and
drive them away. When this occurs, those who flee King
Kragen will have a king of their own, who may eventually . . ." Again his voice paused.

"Who may eventually rival King Kragen in size and
force? The concept is not unreasonable—although King
Kragen is already enormous from long feasting and shows
no signs of halting his growth."

An almost imperceptible tremor moved the floor of the
hut. Blasdel went to look out the door. "I thought I felt
the arrival of a coracle."

"Conceivably a gust of wind," said Berwick. "Well, to
my errand. As you have guessed, I did not come to examine your relicts or comment upon the comfort of your

cottage. My business is this. More than two thousand
folk are leaving the Home Floats, and I feel that no
one, not even the most violently fanatic intercessor, would
wish this group to meet King Kragen upon the ocean.
King Kragen, as you are aware, becomes petulant, even
wrathful, when he finds men trespassing upon his realm.
Now he is more irascible than ever. Perhaps he fears the
possibility of the second King Kragen, concerning which
we speculated. Hence I came to inquire the whereabouts
of King Kragen. In the evening the wind blows west, and
the optimum location for King Kragen would be at Tranque or Thrasneck."

Blasdel nodded sagely. "This, of course, is a question of
fortuity and luck, and certainly the emigrants are putting
their luck to the test. Should King Kragen chance to be
waiting in the west tomorrow evening, and should he spy
the flotilla, his wrath might well be excited, to the
detriment of the expedition."

"And where," inquired Berwick, "was King Kragen at
last notification?"

Barquan Blasdel knit his heavy black eyebrows. "I believe that I saw some winks to the effect that he had been
observed cruising easterly below Adelvine toward Sumber. I might have well misread the flicker—I only
noted the configuration from the corner of my eye—but
such was my understanding."

"Excellent," declared Berwick. "This is good news.
The emigrants should then be able to make their departure safely and without interference."

"So we hope," said Blasdel. "King Kragen, of course,
is subject to unpredictable whims and quirks."

Berwick made a confidential sign. "Sometimes—so
it is rumored—he responds to signals transmitted in some
mysterious manner by the intercessors. Tell me, Barquan
Blasdel, is this the case? We are both notables and together share responsibility for the welfare of Apprise Float.
Is it true then that the intercessors communicate with
King Kragen, as has been alleged?"

"Now then, Arbiter Berwick," said Blasdel, "this is
hardly a pertinent question. Should I answer yes, then

I would be divulging a craft secret. Should I answer no, then it would seem that we intercessors boast of nonexistent capabilities. So you must satisfy yourself with those hypotheses that seem the most profitable."

"Fairly answered," said Phyral Berwick. "However —and in the strictest confidence—I will report to you an amusing circumstance. As you know, at both convocations, I more or less aligned myself with the party of Sklar Hast. I was subsequently accepted into their most intimate counsels. I can inform you with authority—but first, you will assure me of your silence? As under no circumstances would I betray Sklar Hast or compromise the safety of the expedition!"

"Certainly, indeed; my lips are sealed as with fourteen-year-old varnish."

"You will under no circumstances communicate, signal, hint, or imply any element of what I am about to confide, to any person or any thing, the prohibition to include written messages, winks, or any other method of communication?"

Barquan Blasdel gave an uneasy, high-pitched laugh —almost a giggle. "Your charge upon me is not only legalistic—it is portentous in the extreme."

"Do you agree to the provisions?"

"Certainly! I have already assured you of my reticence!"

"Well, then, I take you at your word. This is Sklar Hast's amusing tactic: He has arranged that a group of influential intercessors shall accompany the group. If all goes well, the intercessors live. If not, like all the rest, they will be crushed in the mandibles of King Kragen." And Phyral Berwick, standing back, watched Barquan Blasdel with an attentive gaze. "What do you make of that?"

Blasdel stood rigid, fingering his fringe of black beard. He darted a quick glance toward Berwick. "Which intercessors are to be kidnapped?"

"Aha!" said Berwick. "That, like your response to the question I put to you, is in the nature of a craft secret. I doubt if lesser men will be troubled, but if I were intercessor for Aumerge or Sumber or Quatrefoil or even

Apprise, I believe that I might have cause for caution."

Blasdel stared at Berwick with mingled suspicion and uneasiness. "Do you take this means to warn me? If so, I would thank you to speak less ambiguously. Personally I fear no such attack. Within a hundred feet are three stalwarts, testing my daughters for marriage. A loud call would bring instant help from the float, which is scarcely a stick's throw beyond the garden."

Berwick nodded sagely. "It seems then that you are quite secure."

"Still, I must now hurry to the main float," said Blasdel. "I am expected at the hoodwink tower for an all-float conference, and the evening grows no younger."

Berwick bowed and stood aside. "You will naturally remember to reveal nothing of what I told you, to put forth no oblique warning, to hint nothing—in fact, to make no reference to the matter in any way whatever."

Blasdel made an impatient gesture. "I will say nothing beyond my original intention, to the effect that the villain Sklar Hast obviously knows no moderation and that it behooves all notables and craft masters to guard themselves against some form of final vengeance."

Berwick frowned. "I hardly think you need go quite so far. Perhaps you could phrase it somewhat differently. In this wise: Sklar Hast and his sturdy band take their leave in the morning; now is the last chance for persons so inclined to cast in their lot with the group; however, you hope that all intercessors will remain at their posts."

"Pah!" cried Barquan Blasdel indignantly. "That conveys no sense of imminence! I will say Sklar Hast is desperate; should he decide to take hostages, his diseased mind would select intercessors as the most appropriate' persons!"

Berwick made a firm dissent. "This, I believe, transcends the line I have drawn. My honor is at stake, and I can agree to no announcement which baldly states the certainty as a probability. If you choose to make a jocular reference or perhaps urge that not too many intercessors join the expedition, then all is well. A subtle germ of suspicion has been planted, you have done your duty, and my honor has not been compromised."

"Yes, yes," cried Blasdel. "I agree to anything! But I must hurry to the hoodwink tower. While we quibble Sklar Hast and his bandits are capturing intercessors!"

"And what is the harm there?" inquired Berwick mildly. "You state that King Kragen has been observed from Adelvine proceeding west; hence the intercessors are in no danger and presumably will be allowed to return once Sklar Hast is assured that King Kragen is no longer a danger. Conversely, if the intercessors have betrayed Sklar Hast and given information to King Kragen so that he waits at the far west off Sciona Float, then they deserve to die with the rest. It is justice of the most precise and exquisite balance."

"That is the difficulty," muttered Blasdel, trying to push past Berwick to the door. "I cannot answer for the silence of the other intercessors. Suppose one among them has notified King Kragen? Then a great tragedy ensues."

"Interesting! So you can indeed summon King Kragen when you so desire?"

"Yes, yes, but, mind you, this is a secret. And now—"

"It follows then that you always know the whereabouts of King Kragen. How do you achieve this?"

"There is no time to explain; suffice it to say that a means is at hand."

"Right here? In your workroom?"

"Yes indeed. Now stand aside. After I have broadcast the warning, I will make all clear. Stand aside then!"

Berwick shrugged and allowed Blasdel to run from the cottage, through the garden to the edge of the pad.

Blasdel stopped short at the water's edge. The coracle had disappeared. Where previously Apprise Float had raised its foliage and its hoodwink tower against the dusk, there was now only blank water and blank sky. The pad floated free; urged by the west wind of evening it already had left Apprise Float behind.

Blasdel gave an inarticulate sound of fury and woe. He

turned to find Berwick standing behind him. "What has happened?" Blasdel asked.

"It seems that while we talked, advertisermen cut through the stem of your pad. At least this is my presumption."

"Yes, yes," grated Blasdel. "So much is obvious. What else?"

Berwick shrugged. "It appears that, willy-nilly, whether we like it or not, we are part of the great emigration. Now that such is the case, I am relieved to know that you have a means to determine the whereabouts of King Kragen. Come. Let us make use of this device and reassure ourselves."

Blasdel made a harsh, throaty sound. He crouched and for a moment seemed on the point of hurling himself at Phyral Berwick. From the shadows of the verdure appeared another man. Berwick pointed. "I believe Sklar Hast himself is at hand."

"You tricked me," groaned Barquan Blasdel between clenched teeth. "You have performed an infamous act, which you shall regret."

"I have done no such deed, although it appears that you may well have misunderstood my position. But the time for recrimination is not now. We share a similar problem, which is how to escape the malevolence of King Kragen. I suggest that you now proceed to locate him."

Without a word Blasdel turned, proceeded to his cottage. He entered the main room, with Berwick and Sklar Hast close behind. He crossed to the wall, lifted a panel to reveal an inner room. He brought more lights; all entered. A hole had been cut in the floor and through the pad, the spongy tissue having been painted with a black varnish to prevent its growing together. A tube fashioned from fine yellow stalk perhaps four inches in diameter led down into the water. "At the bottom," said Blasdel curtly, "is a carefully devised horn of exact shape and quality. The end is four feet in diameter and covered with a diaphragm of seasoned and varnished pad-skin. King Kragen emits a sound to which this horn is highly sensitive." He went to the tube, put down his ear, listened, slowly turned the tube around a vertical axis. He shook his head. "I hear nothing. This means that King Kragen is at least ten miles distant. If he is closer I can detect him. He passed to the west early today; presumably he swims somewhere near Vidmar or Leumar or Populous Equity."

Sklar Hast laughed quietly. "Urged there by the intercessors?"

Blasdel gave a sour shrug. "As to that I have nothing to say."

"How, then, do you summon King Kragen?"

Blasdel pointed to a rod rising from the floor, the top of which terminated in a crank. "In the water below is a drum. Inside this drum fits a wheel. When the crank is turned, the wheel, working in resin, rubs against the drum and emits a signal. King Kragen can sense this sound from a great distance—once again about ten miles. Assume he is at, say, Sankston, and is needed at Bickle. The intercessor at The Bandings calls him, until the horn reveals him to be four or five miles distant, whereupon the intercessor at Quatrefoil calls him, then the Hastings intercessor, and so forth until he is within range of the intercessor at Bickle Float."

"I see," said Sklar Hast. "In this fashion Semm Voiderveg called King Kragen to Tranque. Whereupon King Kragen destroyed Tranque Float and killed forty-three persons."

"That is the case."

"And you have the hypocrisy to call us murderers!"

Blasdel once more shrugged and said nothing.

Phyral Berwick said, "Perhaps it is fortunate that Semm Voiderveg is already dead. He would have been selected to accompany the emigration, and his lot would not have been a happy one."

"This is unreasonable!" Barquan Blasdel declared heatedly. "He was as faithful to his convictions as Sklar Hast is to his own! After all, Voiderveg did not enjoy the devastation of Tranque Float. It was his home. Many of those who were killed were his friends. He gave his faith and his trust utterly to King Kragen. And, in return, was killed."

Sklar Hast swung around. "And what of you?"

Blasdel shook his head sadly. "I am a man who thinks at many levels."

Sklar Hast turned away in disgust. He spoke to Berwick. "What should we do with this apparatus? Destroy it? Or preserve it?"

Berwick considered. "We might on some occasion wish to listen for King Kragen. I doubt if we will ever desire to summon him."

Sklar Hast gave a sardonic jerk of his head. "Who knows? To his death perhaps." He turned to Blasdel. "What persons are aboard the float in addition to us?"

"My spouse—in the cottage two roofs along. Three young daughters who weave ornaments for the Star-cursing Festival. Three older daughters who prove themselves to three stalwarts. All are unaware that their pad floats on the deep ocean." His voice quavered. "None wish to become emigrants to a strange line of floats."

Sklar Hast said, "No more do any of the rest of us—but we were forced to choose. I feel no pity for them, or for you. There will be work for all hands. Indeed, we may formulate a new guild: the Kragen-killers. If rumor is accurate, they infest the ocean."

He left the room and went out into the night. Blasdel stood rigid, numbed by the alteration in his circumstances. He slowly turned, cast a rancorous glare at Phyral Berwick, who stolidly returned the gaze. Blasdel gave an angry snort of sheer frustration. He went to listen once more at the detecting horn. Then he also left the room.

Berwick followed and lowered the panel. Both joined Sklar Hast at the edge of the pad, where now several coracles were tied. A dozen men stood in the garden. Sklar Hast turned to Blasdel. "Summon your spouse, your daughters, and those who test them. Explain the circumstances, and gather your belongings. The evening breeze is at hand and blows us west. We journey east."

Blasdel departed, accompanied by Berwick. Sklar Hast

and the others entered the workroom, carried everything of value or utility to the coracles, including the small metal relict, the sixty-one books, the listening horn, and the summoning drum. Then all embarked in the coracles, and Barquan Blasdel's beautiful pad was left to drift solitary upon the ocean.

Chapter 10

Morning came to the ocean and with it the breeze from the west. Sails were rigged and the oarsmen rested. The floats could no longer be seen; the ocean was a ruffled blue mirror in all directions. Sklar Hast lowered Blasdel's horn into the water, listened. Nothing could be heard. Barquan Blasdel did the same and agreed that King Kragen was nowhere near.

There were perhaps six hundred coracles in the flotilla, each carrying from three to six persons, with as much gear, household equipment, and tools as possible, together with sacks of food and water.

Two or three hours after sunrise the breeze died. The sails were lowered and oars alone propelled the coracles. At noon the sun burned brightly down, and awnings were rigged overhead to fend away the glare.

Late in the day several medium-sized floats were seen ahead and slightly to the north. The Home Floats and King Kragen were still too close at hand to make the idea of permanent habitation attractive or feasible, but as the evening breeze would soon be rising, to blow the coracles back to the west, the flotilla headed toward the floats in order to tie up and save the oarsmen the effort of rowing into the wind. After twenty-four hours in the coracles, a chance to disembark, to stretch the legs and walk back and forth would be more than welcome.

With the sun low in the west, shining over the backs of the voyagers, the coracles approached the strange floats. They were similar in general appearance to the

Home Floats, but wild and less ordered, with vegetation rampant, so that the central spike was almost a pyramid of foliage. The breeze, blowing from the floats, brought an odor that astonished Sklar Hast. He called to Roger Kelso, who rowed in a nearby coracle. "Do you smell what I think I smell?"

Roger Kelso tested the air, raised his eyebrows. "I'm not sure. I smell something... Perhaps just rubbish, or a dead fish."

"Perhaps." Sklar Hast, standing in the coracle, looked carefully through the tangle, but could see nothing. Other folk in other coracles likewise had scented the stench from the float and were likewise looking uneasily into the foliage. But nothing moved and no sounds were to be heard. The first coracle nosed up to the edge of the float; the youth in the bow jumped ashore with a stake and painter; others did likewise, and presently all the coracles were tied up, either to the float or to one another.

Not everyone alighted, and those who did remained close to the coracles. Presently one of the young men came upon the source of the odor: an area littered with refuse. Nearby was a charred area, where coals still glowed among ashes and smoldering sponge husks. The floats were inhabited.

"By whom?" whispered Meril Rohan. "Who can they be?".

Sklar Hast called out to the jungle: "Come forth! Show yourselves! We mean no harm!"

There was silence, except for the rustle of the wind in the foliage. The sun was now gone, and the afterglow began to darken over the float.

"Look here!" This was the call of a young niggler who had ventured a few hundred yards around the edge of the float. He came running back, holding an object which he gave to Phyral Berwick: a necklace, or at least a circular cord from which was suspended a number of glossy reddish chunks of metal.

Sklar Hast looked with awe toward the foliage. "Come forth! We wish to speak with you!"

He received no answer.

"Savages, probably filthy and naked," muttered Phyral Berwick. "But they have what we don't have—metal. Where do they get it?"

From the tangle now came a screech, a terrible quavering sound full of rage and menace, and at the same time a number of sticks came hurtling down from the sky.

"We're not welcome," said Sklar Hast. "This is clear. Back to our boats."

The voyagers reembarked, with much more celerity than they had gone ashore. From the foliage came another screech, this time of exultation and mirth, and a series of mad hoots, which raised the hair on the necks of the voyagers.

The coracles were cast off and drifted into the lee of the floats, a hundred yards offshore. In the dusk the voyagers saw a number of pallid shapes emerge from the foliage to run back and forth along the shore, prancing and capering. Their faces and physiognomy could not be discerned.

Sklar Hast rowed his coracle a cautious few yards closer, but was greeted by a new shower of sticks and once again retreated.

Darkness fell, and the coracles waited out the evening breeze. On the float a fire was kindled, and two or three dozen manlike creatures emerged to stand in the flicker.

Roger Kelso called to Sklar Hast across the water: "Somewhere I have read of a group of Second or Third folk who committed unorthodox acts and were 'banished' —a word that well may mean 'sent away.' If so, and if they came in this direction, these must be their descendants."

"It is chilling to contemplate how little is the distance between us and savagery," said Sklar Hast. "Still—they have copper, and we do not."

"How is this?" demanded Rubal Gallager. "Where does it come from?"

No one made response, and all looked back across the dark water at the floats, now silhouetted against the sky.

With the end of dusk and the coming of the constellations the wind died, and once more the flotilla proceeded east, across water calm and smooth. All night some rowed while others slept, until finally the first amber flush to the east brought with it a whisper of the welcome wind from the west. Sails were raised; into the dawn scudded the coracles, over a bright, empty sea.

The second day was like the first, with a brief rain squall halfway through the afternoon, which served to replenish the jugs. Swindlers netted various edible sea-creatures, and while the coracles carried ample food, this demonstrated ability to subsist, if necessary, from the ocean was reassuring, and there was singing and badinage between the coracles.

On the morning of the third day a small kragen was observed. It approached from the north, swimming its lunging breast-stroke, and halted a hundred yards distant to watch the flotilla pass. It twitched its vanes, darted forward, almost as if in an effort to alarm the voyagers, then sank abruptly below the surface. A moment later certain of the swindlers gazing down through a water-box saw it pass below—a great sprawling, writhing shadow. A quarter-mile to the south it surfaced and lay floating quietly, then presently disappeared.

Toward the end of the fourth day a line of floats was observed ahead, as rich and beautiful as the Home Floats, though perhaps half as numerous. From the voyagers came rapturous murmurs. Sklar Hast stood up in his coracle, signaled for a conference, and all the other coracles drew close, to form a great raft drifting and rocking on the water.

Sklar Hast said, "Here are the first floats we have encountered, aside from the floats of the savages. We move slowly. King Kragen can swim three times our speed. In a single day and night—if he so chose, and if he knew our whereabouts—he could come to find us. I feel that we should not consider landing here, but should proceed till we come to at least one other line of floats."

Murmers of disappointment arose, for these floats, lush and heavy with black, green, orange, and gold vegetation, after four days on the ocean, seemed an arcadian vision.

There was discussion, a certain amount of argument, and some grumbling to the effect that King Kragen would never see fit to swim this far, either from curiosity or vindictive rage. Phyral Berwick sided with Sklar Hast, as did most of the caste-elders and guild-masters, and finally amid soft cries of regret the floats were left behind. Again the flotilla sailed out upon the empty sea.

At noon on the sixth day another line of floats was sighted, and all knew that here was to be the new home. All were now happy that the first line had been passed. These were as extensive, as spacious, and even more numerous than the Home Floats, with myriads of the prized small pads upon which a family could build and cultivate to its own taste.

The flotilla landed at a large float near the center of the line. There were no evidences of occupation, by savages or otherwise. The coracles were unloaded and moved to a cove where they could not be seen from the sea.

In the evening, after a festive supper, there was an informal council of the guild-masters and caste-elders.

"Our two immediate problems," said Phyral Berwick, "aside from the inevitable toil of establishing ourselves in comfort and security, are the disposition of our hostages, and our organization. These are both problems of some complexity. The matter of organizing ourselves into a responsible group is perhaps the simplest. The problem is this: Looking around me, I see eight Master Hoodwinks, six Master Larceners, sixteen Master Advertisers, and so on. Naturally all cannot be masters. My suggestion is that the various guild-masters confer and select one of their number as grand-master, by lot, by seniority, or by any other means. Then we can function with more decisiveness. This can be a temporary arrangement at least, until we settle other of the floats.

"Secondly—what of those whom we have with us? What of them? They have served their purpose, but now what? We can't kill them, we can't keep them in a pen, we can't let them return to the Home Floats—at least not yet. We must consider the matter carefully."

All turned to look toward the group of intercessors who sat with their families somewhat to the side. The intercessors themselves evinced glumness and dissatisfaction in varying degrees. The spouses and older children appeared less concerned, while the very young, romping with others of their own age, were in the best of spirits.

Barquan Blasdel, noticing that his case was under discussion, scowled, started to rise, then thought better of it and muttered something to the Parnassus Intercessor Luke Robinet.

Roger Kelso said, "If we could trust them to leave us in peace, then there would be no problem. We could give them coracles, stores, and wish them well. But as sure as we sit here, as soon as they returned to the Home Floats, there would be plots and schemes. Blasdel, for one, would like nothing better than to bring King Kragen across the water to punish us."

"We must destroy the beast," said Sklar Hast in a voice of absolute dedication.

"Easier said than done. Though I expect that long years will pass before King Kragen again ventures near a hoodwink tower."

"In the meantime—the intercessors may not return," said Phyral Berwick. "This is a distasteful situation. The act of placing restraints upon anyone violates our most cherished traditions—but it must be. The question becomes: how to enforce these restraints without inflicting harshness?"

The problem was debated at length, and finally a solution was achieved. Most of the coracles were to be taken to a distant float and hidden, where the intercessors could not find them. Only sufficient coracles to serve the needs of swindlers and blackguards and hooligans, at their respective tasks of fish-swindling, arbor-building, and net-emplacement, would be retained. These would be moved to a location forbidden to the intercessors on pain of incarceration in a withe cage. To guarantee that coracles would not be stolen by night, oars and sails would be impounded in a locked and guarded case. Also

—and this stratagem was propounded in a low voice by Roger Kelso, so that the intercessors might not hear— to the keel of each coracle, below the waterline, a line would be attached. This line would run underneath the float and communicate with an alarm of some kind. When the swindlers used a coracle, they would discreetly ·detach the line, and restore it when they returned. Sklar Hast suggested that four or five young swindlers be appointed to guard the coracles and to make sure that the alarm lines were at all times attached when the coracles were not in use.

The system was accepted as that which imposed the least rigor upon the intercessors. Barquan Blasdel, when the prohibitions were explained, waxed indignant. "First you kidnap us and bundle us across perilous seas, then you perform the infamy of proscribing to our feet certain portions of the float! What do you expect of us?"

"We expect cooperation," said Sklar Hast in the driest of voices. "Also work. Here, on the New Floats, everyone works, including intercessors, because here there is no need for intercession."

"You show no more humility or spiritual sense than a six-barb conger," said Barquan Blasdel evenly.

Sklar Hast shrugged. "Eventually we will kill King Kragen, then you may walk where you will and be humble where you will—but until the loathsome beast settles dead to the ocean's floor, you must keep a circumspect distance between yourself and our coracles."

Barquan Blasdel stared at Sklar Hast a full ten seconds. "You have further designs upon the life of King Kragen?"

"Who knows what the future holds?" said Sklar Hast.

On the following day the great task of altering the wild new float began. Pads at the center of the float were designated for removal, in order to form a lagoon. Nigglers stripped away the surface skin, which would serve a great variety of purposes. The pulp below was cut into strips, which when dry and stiff would serve as insulation and planking, or when plucked and shredded became cushioning, fuel, or an ingredient of the coarse paper pro-

duced by scriveners. The ribs and tubes of the pads
were put aside to season, and the lower membrane, this
of the fine transparent quality suitable for windows, was
taken. Below were the great cantilever ribs, from which
coracle keels and sponge arbors were constructed, and
below this the stems, over which sleeves were now fitted
to extend above the water level. Sap exuding was collected
in buckets, boiled and aged to make varnish. Later, perhaps in a month or two when the sap had stopped flowing, the stem would be cut by advertisermen, stripped
of fiber for ropes and cordage, and woody strips for withe.

The aperture thus left vacant would become the float
lagoon: an anchorage for coracles, a pond for captive
food-fish, a source of scenic delight, and a locale for water
sports.

While the nigglers stripped pad-skin from the future
lagoon, others cleared away waste vegetation, which
was burned for ash. Boys climbed the central spikes with
buckets, to collect pollen from the great fruiting pods,
and this when tested proved to be a quality even finer
and more fragrant than the famed Maudelinda yield,
which was a cause for great pleasure.

As soon as withes had been seasoned, larceners and
felons set to work constructing huts, while the bezzlers,
traditionally the monitors of sanitation, cleanliness, and
the purity of the water supply, constructed reservoirs
to store the afternoon rainfall. At all these tasks the
intercessors, their spouses and children, assisted with
more or less good grace and gradually became divided
into two groups: those who gave over their initial resentment and began to adapt themselves to the new life,
and those others—about half—who would not be reconciled and held themselves dourly aloof. Of the latter group
Barquan Blasdel was the most notable representative, and
he made no secret of his continuing resentment. All were
careful to observe the restraints put upon their movements, and night after night the coracle alarm remained
undisturbed.

One evening Sklar Hast joined Roger Kelso and Meril
Rohan at a bench where they were comparing the Sixty-

one Memoria which had been confiscated from Barquan
Blasdel with those that Meril Rohan had copied for herself. "I presume there are differences?" Sklar Hast asked.

"Indeed," said Kelso. "It's inevitable. The Firsts,
whatever their other talents, had few literary skills;
some of the books contain much repetition and dullness,
others are vainglorious and devote pages to self-encomium.
Others are anxious to explain in great detail the vicissi-
tudes that led to their presence on the Ship of Space.
Some of this, inevitably, is omitted in the copying so
that every new edition, in a sense, becomes a set of analects." He tapped Barquan Blasdel's books. "These are
very old and are the most complete of my experience."
He opened one of the books, looked along the pages. "The
Firsts were, of course, a very mixed group, derived from
a social structure far more complicated than our own.
Apparently they might belong to several different castes
at once. There are hints of this situation that I do not
even profess to understand."

"According to my reading of the Analects," said Sklar
Hast, "all describe the Home Worlds as a place of ma-
niacs."

"We have to take some of this with caution. Never forget that the Firsts were human beings very little different
from ourselves. Some were of the most respected castes
of the Home World society, until, as they explain it, persons in authority turned on them and instituted a savage
persecution, ending, as we know, in our ancestors seizing
control of the Ship of Space and fleeing here."

"It is all very confusing," said Sklar Hast. "None seems
to have much contemporary application. For instance,
they do not tell us how they boiled varnish on the Home
World, or how they propelled their coracles. Do creatures like the kragen infest the Home Worlds? If so,
how do the Home Folk deal with them? Do they kill
them or feed them sponges? The Firsts, to my knowledge,
are silent on these points."

"Evidently they are not overly concerned," said Kelso reflectively. "Otherwise they would have dealt with
these matters at length. There is much that they fail to

make clear. As in our own case, the various castes seemed trained to explicit trades. Especially interesting are the memoirs of James Brunet. Like the others, he professes several castes: Scientist, Forger, Caucasoid. All are extinct among us, as the Forgers have all become scriveners. A part of his Memorium consists of rather conventional exhortations to virtue. But at the beginning of the book he says this." Here Kelso opened a book and read:

"To those who follow us, to our children and grandchildren, we can leave no tangible objects of value. We brought nothing to the world but ourselves and the wreckage of our lives. We will undoubtedly die here—a fate probably preferable to New Ossining, but by no means the destiny any of us had planned for ourselves. There is no way to escape. Of the entire group I alone have a technical education, most of which I have forgotten. And to what end could I turn it? This is a soft world. It consists of ocean, air, sunlight, and seaweed. There is land nowhere. To escape—even if we had the craft to build a new ship, which we do not—we need metal, and metal there is none. Even to broadcast a radio signal we need metal. None . . . no clay to make pottery, no silica for glass, no limestone for concrete, no ore from which to smelt metal. Still, on reflection, all is not hopeless. Ash is similar chemically to fire clay. The shells of foraminifera are silica. Our own bones become a source of lime. A very high-melt, if low-quality, glass could result if the three were fused in the proper proportion. Presumably the ocean carries various salts, but how to extract the metal without electricity? There is iron in our blood: how to extract it? A strange helpless sensation to live on this world where the hardest substance is our own bone! We have, during our lives, taken so many things for granted, and now it seems that no one can evoke something from nothing. . . . This is a problem on which I must think. An ingenious man can work won-

ders, and I, a successful forger—or rather, almost successful—am certainly ingenious."

Roger Kelso paused in his reading. "This is the end of the chapter."

"He seems to have been a man of no great force," mused Sklar Hast. "It is true that metal can be found nowhere, except where the savages contemptuously discard it." On the bench before them was the bit of metal which had once graced the workroom of Barquan Blasdel. Sklar Hast lifted it, hefted it. "Obdurate stuff indeed." He reached for the crude copper necklace that they had found on the wild floats. "Here is the great mystery: Where, how do the savages derive this?"

Roger Kelso heaved a deep sigh, shook his head in perplexity. "Eventually we will learn." He returned to the book. "He writes his next chapter after a lapse of months:

"Before I proceed, I must provide as best I can a picture of the way the universe works, for it is clear that none of my colleagues are in any position to do so, excellent fellows though they are. Please do not suspect me of whimsey: our personalities and social worth undoubtedly vary with the context in which we live."

Here Kelso looked up. "I don't quite understand all of his implications. Does he mean that his colleagues are excellent fellows? Or were not? Why should he say this? His own caste doesn't seem to be the highest. . . . I suppose that the matter is unimportant." He turned the pages. "He now goes into an elaborate set of theorizations regarding the nature of the world, which, I confess, I find overcomplex, even artificial. There is no consistency to his beliefs. Either he knows nothing, or is confused, or the world essentially is inconsistent. He claims that all matter is composed of less than a hundred 'elements,' joined together in 'compounds.' The elements are constructed of smaller entities: 'electrons,' 'protons,' 'neutrons,' and others, which are not necessarily matter, but forces, depending on your point of view. When electrons move, the result is an electric current: a substance or condition—he is not clear here—of great energy and many capabilities. Too much electricity is fatal; in smaller quantities we use it to control our bodies. According to Brunet, all sorts of remarkable things can be achieved with electricity."

"Let us provide ourselves an electric current then," said Sklar Hast. "This may become our weapon against the kragen."

"The matter is not so simple. In the first place, the electricity must be channeled through metal wires."

"Here is metal," said Sklar Hast, examining the fragments before him, "though this is hardly likely to be sufficient."

"The electricity must also be generated," said Kelso. "On the Home Planet this seems to be a complicated process, requiring a great deal of metal."

"Then how do we get metal? Are we so backward that, while even the savages strew it around like sponge-husk, we have none?"

Kelso tilted his head dubiously sidewise. "On other planets there seems to be no problem. Ore is refined and shaped into a great variety of tools. Here we have no ore. In other cases, metals are extracted from the sea, once again using electricity."

Sklar Hast made a sound of disgust. "This is like chasing oneself around a pole. To procure metal, we need electricity. To obtain electricity, metal is required. How does one break into this closed circle? The savages are more adept than we. Do they also wield electricity? Perhaps we should send someone to learn from them."

"Not I," said Kelso. He returned to the book. "Brunet mentions various means to generate electricity. There is the 'voltaic cell,' where two metals are immersed in acid. He describes a means to derive the acid, using rain-water, sea-brine, and electricity. Then there is thermoelectricity, photoelectricity, chemical electricity, electricity produced by cataphoresis, electricity generated by moving a wire near another wire in which electricity flows. He states that all living creatures produce small quantities of electricity."

"What of metal?" asked Sklar Hast. "Does he indicate any simple methods to secure metal?"

Kelso turned pages, paused to read. "He mentions that blood contains a small quantity of iron. He suggests a method for extracting it, by using a high degree of heat. But he also points out that there is at hand no substance capable of serving as a receptacle under such extremes of heat. He states that on the Home World many plants concentrate metallic compounds, and suggests that certain of our own sea-plants might do the same. But again either heat or electricity is needed to secure the pure metal."

Sklar Hast ruminated. "Our first and basic problem, as I see it, is self-protection. We need a weapon to kill King Kragen in the event that he tracks us across the sea. It might be a device of metal—or it might be a larger and more savage kragen, if such exist. . . ." He considered. "Perhaps you should make production of metal and electricity your goal, and let no other pursuits distract you. I am sure that the council will agree and put at your disposal such helpers as you may need."

"I would be pleased to do my best."

"And I," said Sklar Hast, "I will reflect upon the kragen."

Chapter 11

Three days later a kragen was seen, a beast of not inconsiderable size, perhaps twenty feet in length. It came cruising along the edge of the float and, observing the men, stopped short. For twenty minutes it floated placidly, swirling water back and forth with its vanes. Then slowly it swung about and continued along the line of floats.

A month passed, during which the community achieved a rude measure of comfort. A large quantity of stalk and withe had been cut, scraped and racked. A rope-walk had been rigged, and root-wisp was being twisted into rope. Three large pads had been cut from the side and center of the float, creating a large lagoon with a relatively narrow mouth—this at the request of Sklar Hast. Arbors were constructed, seeded with sponge-floss, and lowered into the water.

During this period four kragen had passed by. The fourth occurrence seemed to be a return visit of the first. On this fourth visit the kragen paused, inspected the lagoon with care. It tentatively nudged the net, which had just been set in place, then backed away and presently floated off.

Sklar Hast watched the occurrence. Then he went to inspect the new-cut stalk, which now was sufficiently cured. He laid out a pattern, and work began. First a wide base was built near the narrow mouth of the lagoon, with a substructure extending down to the main stem of the float. On this base was erected an A-frame derrick of

126

glued withe, seventy feet tall, with integral braces, the entire structure whipped tightly with strong line and varnished. Another identical derrick was built to overhang the ocean. Before either of the derricks were completed, a small kragen broke through the net to feast upon the yet unripe sponges. "At your next visit, you will not fare so well," Sklar Hast called to the beast. "May the sponges rot in your stomach!"

The kragen swam lazily off down the line of floats, unperturbed by the threat. It returned two days later. This time the derricks were guyed and in place, but not yet fitted with tackle. Again Sklar Hast reviled the beast, which this time ate with greater fastidiousness, plucking only those sponges which like popcorn had overgrown their husks. The men worked far into the night installing the strut which, when the derrick tilted out over the water, thrust high the topping-halyard to provide greater leverage.

On the next day the kragen returned and entered the lagoon with insulting assurance, a beast somewhat smaller than that which Sklar Hast had captured on Tranque Float, but nonetheless a creature of respectable size. Standing on the float, a stalwart old swindler flung a noose around the creature's turret, and on the pad a line of fifty men marched away with a heavy rope. The astonished kragen was towed to the outward-leaning derrick, swung up and in. The dangling vanes were lashed; it was lowered to the float.

As soon as the bulk collapsed, the watching folk, crying out in glee, shoved forward, almost dancing into the gnashing mandibles. "Back, fools!" roared Sklar Hast. "Do you want to be cut in half? Back!"

He was largely ignored. A dozen chisels hacked at the horny hide; clubs battered at the eyes. "Back!" raged Sklar Hast. "Back! What do you achieve by antics such as this? Back!"

Daunted, the vengeful folk moved aside. Sklar Hast took chisel and mallet and, as he had done on Tranque Float, cut at the membrane joining dome to turret. He was joined by four others; the channel was swiftly cut,

and a dozen hands ripped away the dome. Again, with
pitiless outcry, the crowd surged forward. Sklar Hast's
efforts to halt them were fruitless. The nerves and cords
of the creature's ganglionic center were torn from the
turret, while the kragen jerked and·fluttered and made
a buzzing sound with its mandibles. The turret was
plucked clean of the wet-string fibers as well as other organs, and the kragen lay limp.

Sklar Hast moved away in disgust. Rollo Barnack
jumped up on the hulk. "Halt now! No more senseless
hacking! If the kragen has bones harder than our own,
we will want to preserve them for use. Who knows what
use can be made of a kragen's cadaver? The hide is
tough; the mandibles are harder than the deepest stalk.
Let us proceed intelligently!"

Sklar Hast watched from a little distance as the crowd
examined the dead beast. He had no further interest in
the kragen. A planned experiment had been foiled almost
as soon as the hate-driven mob had rushed forward. But
there would be more kragen for his derricks; hopefully
they could be noosed by the sea-derrick before they
broke into the lagoon. In years to come, strong-boats or
barges equipped with derricks might even go forth to
hunt the kragen.... He approached the kragen once
again, peered into the empty turret, where now welled a
puddle of viscous dark blue blood. The sight stirred
something deep in his brain: a response, a recollection,
a reference. In the Analects? It came to him: The blood
of certain sea-creatures of Earth also ran blue: lobsters
and king crab, whatever these might be.

Kelso shared a similar interest in the dark blue fluid.
He brought buckets with which he bailed out the blood
and conveyed it to a barrel. Sklar Hast watched with
interest. "What do you propose?"

"Nothing definite. I am collecting substances. The savages found metal somewhere. If I collect enough materials and try various methods of extraction on all, perhaps
I will be able to achieve what the savages have already
done."

"The savages are proving a great inspiration," said

Sklar Hast. "I wonder what other wonders and accomplishments they could teach?"

"Here would be a good use to make of the intercessors," observed Rollo Barnack. "So far they have showed little enthusiasm for the new life."

"The death of the kragen has made them very glum," said Wall Bunce jocularly. "Hey, intercessors! What do you think now?"

The intercessors, who had watched the killing of the kragen from a distance, turned away in contempt and disgust. Sklar Hast strolled over to where they stood talking in low voices. "Do you still think that we need fear harassment by the kragen?" he asked.

Luke Robinet spoke in a voice quivering with detestation. "These are small fry and not King Kragen. Someday he will find you and punish you for breaking the Covenant. Then all your ropes and pulleys and derricks will be of no avail whatever!"

Sklar Hast nodded dolefully. "It would be a sad affair. King Kragen should have been killed when he first appeared, as we have killed the sea-beast today. Think how much easier life would have been for all of us! Instead he was fed and fawned upon, and now he looms over all our lives."

Barquan Blasdel said in his even, easy voice: "You are an insensitive man, Sklar Hast. You see only what is before your nose; you are ignorant of the spiritual benefits to be derived from self-abasement."

"Absolutely true," said Sklar Hast. "I fear I have suffered serious disadvantages in this respect."

The Wyebolt Intercessor, a thin, hot-eyed old man with an undisciplined mop of white hair, rasped: "Your sarcastic fleers and flaunts will avail little when King Kragen at last demands an accounting!"

Sklar Hast noted certain uneasy movements and grimaces among the intercessors. "How do you expect that this will come to pass?"

The Wyebolt Intercessor ignored the wry looks of his fellows, or perhaps, sensing them, he modified his reply. "What will be, will be. It certainly must be assumed that

King Kragen will not allow his intercessors to be so misused."

"The beast neither knows nor cares," scoffed Sklar Hast, hoping to infuriate the Wyebolt Intercessor to the point where he might make an indiscreet revelation.

Barquan Blasdel performed a large, almost indulgent gesture. "This conversation is bootless. You have us at a disadvantage. Eventually these poor folk will tire of your crass materialism and reject all that you represent. Until then we must be patient." With a quick but monitory glance around the circle of intercessors, he crossed to his hut and disappeared within.

Sklar Hast moved on, across the float to where Meril Rohan had established what she called a "school" for the instruction of children. This was an institution not absolutely unknown on the Home Floats—in fact, the Quatrefoil Academy for the training of scriveners was notable—but children usually were educated through guild agencies.

Meril had watched the landing of the kragen but had taken no part in the frenzied death-rite. Instead, turning her back, she had gone to her "school", which, of course, had been vacated by reason of the excitement at the other side of the float.

Here Sklar Hast, coming through the still heavy tangle of vines, found her, sitting on a bench looking out across the blue water. He approached and sat beside her. "What are you thinking about?"

She was silent a moment. "I was thinking about the times to come, and wondering what is to befall us."

Sklar Hast laughed. "I can't allow myself to wonder. The problems of Now are too great. If I wondered where all was to lead, I'd be halted."

Meril, making no reply, nodded slowly as if at some profound inner discovery.

"And where does all your wondering take you?" Sklar Hast asked.

"No single place. We are of the Eleventh generation; already there are Twelfths and Thirteenths. It seems that over all these years we have been living dreams. The

Floats were so easy and fertile that no one has ever been forced to work or think or suffer. Or fight."

Sklar Hast nodded gloomily. "Undoubtedly you are right—but now we have been forced, and we are fighting. Today we won our first victory."

"But such a cheap victory. And what is the fight for? Merely that the kragen should not eat our sponges, that we should be allowed to continue this dreaming placid life, that it might go on forever. . . . I am not proud of myself. I was sickened by the death of the kragen. We fled the Home Floats. It was the right thing to do—but is this the end of our ambitions? A life of lagoons and sunlight, without even King Kragen to worry us? It frightens me somehow, and I wonder if this is all my life is to be: something without achievement or victory or meaning of any kind whatever."

Sklar Hast frowned. "I have never thought exactly in these terms. Always the immediate problems seem urgent."

"I imagine that this would always be the case, no matter how trivial the problems. In her Memorium Eleanor Morse speaks of her 'goals,' and how they moved further and further into the distance, and so to achieve them she forced herself to become a Bezzler. This has no particular meaning for us, except that it illustrates how ambition forces folk to better themselves. So I have been trying to form some goals for myself, that I might just possibly hope to achieve."

"What are they?"

"You won't mock me? Or laugh?" Meril turned grave eyes upon him.

"No." Sklar Hast took her hand, held it.

Meril looked around the array of crude benches. "I attended the Scriveners' Academy on Quatrefoil. There are four large structures furnished for study, a refectory, and two dormitories. I want to bring such an academy into being here. Not just a place for scriveners, but an academy for the advancement of all knowledge. There are hints of what is to be learned in the Memoria. . . . This is my goal: to establish this academy, where the

young people learn their guild skills, learn the Memoria,
but, most important, learn the same dissatisfaction that I
feel, so that they, too, shall have goals."

Sklar Hast was silent. Then he said, "You shall certainly have all my help. . . . And you shame me. I ask myself, what are my own goals? I am sorry to say that they
were satisfied, at least in part, when the derrick lifted
the kragen from the water. I had thought no farther
ahead. True, I want this float to be prosperous and
happy. . . ." He frowned. "I have a goal. Two goals.
First: I want you for my spouse. I want no other. Second:
I want to destroy King Kragen." He took her other hand.
"What do you say to this?"

"Destroy King Kragen, by all means."

"And what of the first goal?"

"I would think it is—attainable."

A hand shook Sklar Hast. He awoke to see a dark form
standing above him, black against the stars. "Who is it?
What do you want?"

"I am Julio Rile; I guard the coracles. I want you to
come with me."

Sklar Hast lurched to his feet, pulled on a cloak, slipped
his feet into sandals. "What happens? Are they stealing
our boats?"

"No. There is a strange noise coming from the water."

Sklar Hast went with the youth to the edge of the float.
Kneeling, putting his head close to the water, he heard
a groaning, scraping, wheezing sound, unlike any that
he had ever heard before. There was one that had been
similar. . . . Sklar Hast turned, went at a lope to the hut
that housed the horn taken from Barquan Blasdel's pad
at Apprise Float. He brought it forth, carried it to the
edge of the float, lowered it into the water. The sound
was startlingly loud. Sklar Hast turned the horn, noted
the direction from which the sound reached a maximum
intensity. He grinned a sudden angry grin. "Go, wake
Phyral Berwick and Rollo Barnack and Rubal Gallager.
Make haste. Bring them here."

Sklar Hast awoke Poe Belrod and Roger Kelso. The

whole group listened at the horn and looked in the direction from which the sound seemed to emanate: the hut occupied by Barquan Blasdel.

Sklar Hast whispered: "Someone will be watching at the front; let us approach from the back."

They moved quietly through the shadows, around to the rear of Barquan Blasdel's hut. Sklar Hast brought out a knife. He slit the pad-skin, pushed through into the interior.

A lamp on a shelf lit the room dimly. Kneeling around a hole in the floor were Barquan Blasdel and Luke Robinet. They manipulated a contrivance of wood, leather, and cord, which extended through the hole into the black water. To the side was a plug to fill the hole during the day.

Barquan Blasdel slowly rose to his feet, as did Luke Robinet. Into the room came Phyral Berwick, Roger Kelso, and the others.

No one spoke. There was clearly nothing to, be said. Sklar Hast went to the hole, lifted out the sound-producing mechanism, replaced the plug.

There were hurried footsteps in the outer room. A voice spoke through the door. "Caution; halt the sounds. Folk are astir."

Sklar Hast flung wide the door, seized the speaker, Vidal Reach, formerly Sumber Intercessor, and drew him into the room. Quietly he went to the front door. No one else could be seen. In all likelihood the entire group of intercessors were concerned with the plot, but only these three could be directly charged.

From the first Barquan Blasdel had made no pretense of satisfaction with his altered circumstances. His former rank counted nothing, and in fact aroused antagonism among his float-fellows. Blasdel grudgingly adapted himself to his new life, building sponge-arbors and scraping withe. His spouse, who on Apprise Float had commanded a corps of four maidens and three garden-men, at first rebelled when Blasdel required her to bake pangolay, as the bread-stuff baked from pollen was known, and core sponges "like any low-caste slut," as she put it. Finally she surrendered to the protests of her empty stomach. Her daughters adapted themselves with better grace, and indeed the four youngest participated with great glee at the slaughter of the kragen. The remaining two stayed in the background, eyebrows raised at the vulgar fervor of their sisters.

These then were the circumstances of Barquan Blasdel's existence at the time of his ill-founded concept of summoning King Kragen. Luke Robinet and Vidal Reach lived under similar conditions, with no restraints except in regard to the coracles.

On the morning after their apprehension, the three conspirators were brought before a judicial assembly of guild-masters and caste-elders. Inasmuch as Phyral Berwick had participated in the actual apprehension of the persons accused, Gian Recargo served as Arbiter.

The morning sun shone bright on the float. At the entrance to the lagoon lay the bulk of the kragen, still in the process of being flensed by apprentice nigglers and advertisers. The assembly sat in near silence, conversing in whispers.

From the hut where they had spent the night came Barquan Blasdel, Luke Robinet, and Vidal Reach, blinking in the glare of the sun. In utter silence they were marched to a bench and ordered to sit.

Phyral Berwick arose and described the circumstances of the previous night. "It is evident that they intended to attract the attention of King Kragen, if by some chance he was cruising near."

Gian Recargo leaned forward. "Have they admitted as much?"

The Arbiter looked at the accused. "What have you to say?"

"So far as I am concerned, nothing," said Barquan Blasdel.

"You admit the charges?"

"I have no statement to make. Things are as they are."

"Do you deny or repudiate any of Phyral Berwick's testimony?"

"No."

"You must be aware that this is an extremely serious charge."

"From your point of view."

"Did you have reason to believe that King Kragen is, or was, in the vicinity? Or did you produce this noise merely in the hope of attracting his attention if he should chance to be nearby?"

"I repeat, I have no statement to make."

"You put forward no defense?"

"It would obviously be futile."

"You do not deny the acts?"

"I have no statement to make. Things are as they are."

Luke Robinet and Vidal Reach were similarly taciturn. The Arbiter took statements from Sklar Hast, Julio Rile, and Rollo Barnack. He said, "Clearly the accused are guilty of the most vindictive intentions. I am at a loss as to what penalty to impose. There is absolutely no precedent, to my knowledge."

Phyral Berwick spoke. "Our problem is how to make ourselves secure. We can kill these men. We might maroon them on a lonely float, even the Savage Floats, or we can guard them more carefully. I even feel a certain sympathy for them. If I shared the fervor of their convictions, I might act similarly in a similar situation. I say, give them the sternest of warnings, but give them their lives."

No one dissented. Gian Recargo turned to the three criminals. "We give you your lives. All shall be as before. I suspect that this is more than you would do for us, but no matter. We are not you. But remember, for our own security, we can show no more mercy! Consider that you are now living a new life, and make the best possible use of it. Go. Return to your work. Try to make yourselves deserving of the trust we have placed in you."

"We did not ask to be brought here," said Barquan Blasdel in his easy voice.

"Your presence here is a direct consequence of your original treachery, when you attempted to arrange that King Kragen should intercept our flotilla. In retrospect, it seems that we are unreasonably merciful. Still, this is the nature of the life we hope to lead—and you are the unworthy beneficiaries. Go, and remember that mercy will not be extended a third time."

Luke Robinet and Vidal Reach were somewhat subdued, but Barquan Blasdel sauntered away undaunted. Sklar Hast and Roger Kelso watched him depart. "There is a man who knows only hate," said Sklar Hast. "Forbearance has not won his gratitude. He will bear the most vigilant watch!"

"We are not preparing ourselves fast enough," said Kelso.

"For what?"

"For the inevitable confrontation. Sooner or later King Kragen will find us. The intercessors seem to feel that he swims this far afield. If he comes, we have no means of escape, and certainly no means to repel him."

Sklar Hast somberly agreed. "All too true. We do not feel enough urgency; this is indeed a false security. By some means we must formulate a system by which we can protect ourselves. Weapons! Think of a great harpoon, launched by a hundred men, tipped with hard metal . . . But we have no metal."

"But we do," said Kelso. He brought forth a gray pellet the size of a baby's tooth. "This is iron."

Sklar Hast took it, turned it back and forth in his fingers. "Iron! From where did it come?"

"I produced it."

"By the system the savages use?"

"As to that, I can't say."

"But how? What is its source? The air? The sea? The fruit of the float?"

"Come to Outcry Float tomorrow, somewhat before noon. I will explain all."

"Including the provenance of the name 'Outcry'?"

"All will be explained."

Chapter 12

In order to work undisturbed, with a minimum of interference from casual passers-by and elderly guild-masters with well-meant advice, Kelso had preempted for
his investigations the float next to the west, and this, for
reasons arising from his activities, became known as
Outcry Float. For helpers and assistants and fellow re-
searchers, Kelso had recruited several dozen of the most
alert young men and women available, who worked with
an energy and enthusiasm surprising even to themselves.

Only three hundred yards separated the two floats, and
as Sklar Hast paddled the intervening distance, he already envisaged hoodwink towers transmitting messages
between the two. A vagrant thought came to him: Best
set up practice machines, so that old hoodwinks should
not lose their reflexes, that apprentices might be instructed, that the craft might be kept alive.

Arriving at Outcry Float, he tied the coracle to the
rude dock which Kelso had caused to be built. A path
led around a tall clump of banner-bush into a central
area beside the central spike, which was now scrupulously
cleared of vegetation, and as a result the pad surface
had become a liverish purple-brown.

Kelso was hard at work on an intricate contrivance
the purpose of which Sklar Hast could not fathom. A
rectangular frame of stalk rose ten feet in the air, supporting a six-foot hoop of woven withe in a plane parallel
to the surface of the float. To the hoop was glued a large
sheet of first-quality pad-skin, which had been scraped,

137

rubbed, and oiled until it was almost perfectly transparent. Below, Kelso now arranged a box containing ashes. As Sklar Hast watched, he mixed in a quantity of water and some gum, enough to make a gray dough, which he worked with his fingers and knuckles, to leave a saucer-shaped depression.

The sun neared the zenith; Kelso signaled two of his helpers. One climbed the staging; the other passed up buckets of water. The first poured these upon the transparent membrane, which sagged under the weight.

Sklar Hast watched silently, giving no voice to his perplexity. The membrane, now brimming, seemed to bulge perilously. Kelso, at last satisfied with his arrangements, joined Sklar Hast. "You are puzzled by this device; nevertheless it is very simple. You own a telescope?"

"I do. An adequately good instrument, though the gum is clouded."

"The purest and most highly refined gum discolors, and even with the most careful craftsmanship lenses formed of gum yield distorted images, of poor magnification. On the Home World, according to Brunet, lenses are formed of a material called 'glass.' "

The sun reached the zenith; Sklar Hast's attention was caught by a peculiar occurrence in the box of damp ash. A white-hot spot had appeared; the ash began to hiss and smoke. He drew near in wonderment. "Glass would seem a useful material," Kelso was saying. "Brunet describes it as a mixture of substances occurring in ash which he calls 'fluxes,' together with a compound called 'silica' which is found in ash, but also occurs in husks of sea-ooze: 'plankton,' as Brunet calls it. Here I have mixed ash and sea-ooze; I have constructed a water-lens to condense sunlight. I am trying to make glass. . . ."

He peered into the box, then lifted it a trifle, bringing the image of the sun to its sharpest focus. The ash glowed red, orange, yellow; suddenly it seemed to slump. With a rod Kelso pushed more ash into the center, until the wooden box gave off smoke, whereupon Kelso pulled it aside and gazed anxiously at the molten matter in the center. "Something has happened; exactly what we will determine when the stuff is cool."

He turned to his bench, brought forward another box, this half-full of powdered charcoal. In a center depression rested a cake of black-brown paste.

"And what do you have there?" asked Sklar Hast, already marveling at Kelso's ingenuity.

"Dried blood. I and my men have drained ourselves pale. It is an operation conducive of woe, hence 'Outcry Float.'"

"But why should you bleed yourself?" demanded Sklar Hast.

"Again I must refer you to the scientist Brunet. He reveals that human blood is colored red by a substance called 'hemoglobin.' This is composed of much carbon, oxygen, and hydrogen and a single particle of iron. Carbon is the main ingredient of char; oxygen gives to air its invigorating quality; with hydrogen oxygen makes water. But today we seek only that extremely small quantity of iron. So here is blood. I will burn away the various unstable fluids, gases, and oozes, to discover what remains. If all goes well, we will again find unyielding iron." Kelso thrust the box under the lens. The dried blood smoldered and smoked, then burst into flame which gave off a nauseous odor. Kelso squinted up at the sun. "The lens burns well only when the sun is overhead, so our time is necessarily limited."

"Rather than water, transparent gum might be used, which then would harden, and the sun could be followed across the sky."

"Unfortunately no gum is so clear as water," said Kelso regretfully. "Candle-plant sap is yellow. Bindle-bane seep holds a blue fog."

"What if the two were mixed, so that the blue defeated the yellow? And then the two might be filtered and boiled. Or perhaps water can be coagulated with tincture of bone."

Kelso assented. "Possibly feasible, both."

They turned to watch the blood, now a glowing sponge which tumbled into cinders and then, apparently con-

sumed, vanished upon the surface of the blazing charcoal. Kelso snatched the crucible out from under the lens.
"Your blood seems not overrich," Sklar Hast noted
critically. "It might be wise to tap Barquan Blasdel and
the intercessors; they appear a hearty lot."

Kelso clapped a cover upon the box. "We will know
better when the charcoal goes black." He went to his
bench, brought back another box. In powdered charcoal stood another tablet, this of black paste. "And
what substance is this?" inquired Sklar Hast.

"This," said Kelso, "is kragen blood, which we boiled
last night. If man's blood carries iron, what will kragen
blood yield? Now we discover." He thrust it under the
lens. Like the human blood, it began to smolder and
burn, discharging a smoke even more vile than before.
Gradually the tablet flaked and tumbled to the surface
of the charcoal; as before, Kelso removed it and covered
it with a lid. Going to his first box, he prodded among the
cinders with a bit of sharp bone, scooped out a congealed
puddle of fused material which he laid on the bench.
"Glass. Beware. It is yet hot."

Sklar Hast, using two pieces of bone, lifted the object.
"So this is glass. Hmm. It hardly seems suitable for use
as a telescope lens. But it may well prove useful otherwise. It seems dense and hard—indeed, almost metallic."

Kelso shook his head in deprecation. "I had hoped for
greater transparency. There are probably numerous im-
purities in the ash and sea-ooze. Perhaps they can be removed by washing the ash or treating it with acid, or
something of the sort."

"But to produce acid, electricity is necessary, or so
you tell me."

"I merely quote Brunet."

"And electricity is impossible?"

Kelso pursed his lips. "That we will see. I have hopes.
One might well think it impossible to generate electricity
using only ash, wood, water, and sea-stuff—but we shall
see. Brunet offers a hint or two. But first, as to our iron . . .'

The yield was small: a nodule of pitted gray metal
like the first, half the size of a pea. "That bit represents

three flasks of blood," Kelso remarked glumly. "If we bled every vein on the float, we might win sufficient iron for a small pot."

"This is not intrinsically an unreasonable proposal," said Sklar Hast. "We can all afford a flask of blood or two, or even more, during the course of months. To think —we have produced metal entirely on our own resources!"

Kelso wryly inspected the iron nodule. "There is no problem to burning the blood under the lens. If every day ten of the folk come to be bled, eventually we will sink the pad under the accumulated weight of the iron." He removed the lid from the third box. "But observe here! We have misused our curses! The kragen is by no means a creature to be despised!"

On the charcoal rested a small puddle of reddish-golden metal, three times as large as the iron nodule. "This metal must be copper, or one of its alloys. Brunet describes copper as a dark red metal, very useful for the purpose of conducting electricity."

Sklar Hast lifted the copper from the coals, tossed it back and forth till it was cool. "The savages have copper, in chunks larger than this. Do they kill kragen and burn their blood? It seems incredible! Those distorted furtive half-men!"

Kelso chewed reflectively at his lip. "The kragen must ingest its copper from some source. Perhaps the savages know the source."

"Metal!" murmured Sklar Hast reverently. "Metal everywhere! Nicklas Rile has been hacking apart the kragen for its bones. He is discarding the internal organs, which are black as snuff-flower. Perhaps they should also be burned under the lens."

"Convey them here—I will burn them. And then, after we burn the kragen's liver or whatever the organ, we might attempt to burn snuff-flower as well. Who knows? Perhaps all black substances yield copper, all red substances iron. Though Brunet never makes so inclusive a generalization."

The kragen's internal organs yielded further copper. The snuff-flowers produced only a whitish-yellow ash which Kelso conscientiously stored in a tube labeled: "Ash of a Snuff-flower."

Four days later the largest kragen seen so far appeared. It came swimming in from the west, paralleling the line of floats. A pair of swindlers, returning to the float with a catch of gray-fish, were the first to spy the great black cylinder surmounted by its four-eyed turret. They bent to their oars, shouting the news ahead.

A well-rehearsed plan now went into effect. A team of four young swindlers ran to a lightweight coracle, shoved off, paddled out to intercept the kragen. Behind the coracle trailed two ropes, each controlled by a gang of men. The kragen, lunging easily through the water, approached, swimming fifty yards off the float. The coracle eased forward, rowed by two of the men, with one named Bade Beach going forward to stand on the gunwales. The kragen stopped the motion of its vanes, to drift and eye the coracle and the derricks with flinty suspicion.

The two swindlers at the oars thrust the coracle closer. Bade Beach stood tensely, twitching a noose. The fourth man controlled the lines to the float. The kragen, contemptuous of attack, issued a few nonplused clicks of the mandibles, twitched the tips of its vanes, to create four whirlpools. The coracle eased closer, to within 100 feet—80—60 feet. Bade Beach bent forward.

The kragen decided to punish the men for their provocative actions. It thrust sharply forward. When it was but 30 feet distant, Bade Beach tossed a noose toward the turret—and missed. From the float came groans of disappointment. One of the gangs hastily jerked the coracle back. The kragen swerved, turned, made a second furious charge which brought it momentarily to within five feet of the coracle, whereupon Bade Beach dropped the noose over its turret. From the float came a cheer; both gangs hauled on their lines, one snatching the coracle back to safety, the other tightening the noose and pulling the kragen aside, almost as it touched the coracle.

Thrashing and jerking, the kragen was dragged over

to the sea-leaning derrick and hoisted from the water in the same fashion as the first. This was a large beast; the derrick creaked, the float sagged before the kragen heaved clear from the water, 65 men were tugging on the end of the lift. The derrick tilted back; the kragen swung in over the float. The vanes were lashed, the beast lowered. Again the onlookers surged forward, laughing, shouting, but no longer manifesting the fury with which they had attacked the first kragen.

Chisels and mallets were plied against the kragen turret; the dome was pried loose, the nerve-nodes destroyed. Fiber buckets were brought; the body fluids were scooped out and carried off to evaporation trays.

Sklar Hast had watched from the side. This had been a large beast—about the size of King Kragen when first he had approached the Old Floats, a hundred and fifty years previously. Since they had successfully dealt with this creature, they need have small fear of any other— except King Kragen. And Sklar Hast was forced to admit that the answer was not yet known. No derrick could hoist King Kragen from the water. No line could restrain the thrust of his vanes. No float could bear his weight. Compared to King Kragen, this dead hulk was a pygmy
. . . .

From behind came a rush of feet; a woman tugged at his elbow, gasping and gulping in the effort to catch her breath. Sklar Hast, startled, scanning the float, could see nothing to occasion her distress. Finally she was able to blurt: "Barquan Blasdel has taken to the sea, Barquan Blasdel is gone!"

"What!" cried Sklar Hast.

Chapter 13

Barquan Blasdel, his spouse, his two older daughters and their lovers, together with Luke Robinet and Vidal Reach, were missing, as was a sturdy coracle. Their plans had been daring, carefully laid and precisely executed. For weeks they had secreted stores in a tangled nook to the far side of the float, near Meril Rohan's school. Secretly oars, a mast, and a sail had been fabricated. Then they had awaited the capture of a second kragen, assuming correctly that the attention of everyone would be diverted.

The two young men, spouses to Blasdel's daughters, made off with the coracle. Even with a kragen dangling in mid-air, the sight of Barquan Blasdel in a coracle might well have attracted attention. The two young men were more inconspicuous. They untied the coracle, paddled it around to the south side of the float. The stores were loaded aboard, all embarked, oars were shipped and the coracle sent scudding away from New Home Float. By sheer bad luck a woman rendered squeamish by pregnancy had put the breadth of the float between her and the landing of the kragen, and had seen the coracle disappearing around Outcry Float.

Phyral Berwick dispatched ten coracles in instant pursuit, but by this time evening was at hand, with an unusually brisk wind. What with the sail, all hands at the oars, the dusk; and dozens of floats to hide among, there was small chance that the fugitive coracle could be overtaken. Barquan Blasdel might even choose to veer north or south and so lose himself the more completely.

The search coracles stayed out all night. Eight searched among the floats, ghosting back and forth along the starlit channels; two struck west as fast and hard as the most stalwart swindlers could take them. When dawn came to throw a pearl-colored light over the sea, the new floats were almost invisible to the east, but the searchers were alone on the sea. Barquan Blasdel's coracle was nowhere to be seen. Those searching among the floats fared no better. All returned to New Home Float on the dawn wind.

A convocation of the councilors was called to consider the situation. Some bemoaned the leniency which had been extended the fugitive intercessors. "Why did we allow our qualms to conquer us?" moaned Robin Magram. "We should have made a clean job and strangled the lot."

Phyral Berwick nodded patiently. "You may be right. Still, I for one could not bring myself to commit murder, even though it would have been to our best interests."

Magram jerked his thumb toward the huts in which lurked the remaining intercessors. "What of them? Each wishes us evil. Each is now planning the same despicable act as that performed by Blasdel. Let us kill them now— quietly, without malice, but with a beautiful finality!"

Sklar Hast made a morose objection. "This would do no good. We would become murderers in all truth. The fat is now in the fire. In fact, we would do better by turning them free—giving them a coracle and sending them off."

"Not so fast!" protested Rollo Barnack. "Barquan Blasdel may never reach the Home Floats!"

"He need merely sail on the night wind and paddle west," said Sklar Hast. "But very well, let us wait till we know for sure what has eventuated."

Robin Magram growled, "If Barquan Blasdel returns to the old floats, one eventuation is sure. We must expect hostile actions. The man is a vessel of malice."

"Not necessarily," argued Phyral Berwick. "Remember, the folk of the floats are by and large sensible. They are our caste-brothers, our friends, our relatives. And what do they gain by attacking us?"

"We have escaped King Kragen; we acknowledge no overlord," said Sklar Hast pessimistically. "Misery brings jealousy and resentment. The intercessors can whip them to a sullen fury." He pitched his voice to a nasal falsetto. " 'Those insolent fugitives! How dare they scamp their responsibility to noble King Kragen? How dare they perform such bestial outrages against the lesser kragen? Everyone to the coracles! We go to punish the iconoclasts!' "

"Possibly correct," said Kelso. "But the intercessors are by no means the only influential folk of the floats. The arbiters will hardly agree to any such schemes."

"In essence," said Phyral Berwick, "we have no information. We speculate in a void. Barquan Blasdel may lose himself on the ocean and never return to the Old Floats. He may be greeted with apathy or with excitement. We talk without knowledge. It seems to me that we should take steps to inform ourselves as to the true state of affairs—in short, that we send spies to derive this information for us."

Phyral Berwick's proposal ultimately became the decision of all. It was further decided that the remaining intercessors be guarded more carefully, until it was definitely learned whether or not Barquan Blasdel had returned to the Old Floats. If such were the case, the location of the New Floats was no longer a secret, and the consensus was that the remaining intercessors should likewise be allowed to return, should they choose to do so. Robin Magram considered the decision soft-headed. "Do you think they would warrant us like treatment in a similar situation? Remeber, they planned that King Kragen should waylay us!"

"True enough," said Arrel Sincere wearily, "but what of that? We can either kill them, hold them under guard, or let them go their way, the last option being the least taxing and the most honorable."

Robin Magram made no further protest, and the council then concerned itself with the details of the pro-

jected spy operation. None of the coracles at hand were
considered suitable, and it was decided to build a coracle of special design—long, light, low to the water, with
two sails of fine weave to catch every whisper of wind.
Three men were named to the operation, all originally
of Almack Float, a small community far to the east, in
fact next to Sciona, at the end of the chain. None of the
three had acquaintance on Apprise and so stood mini-
mal chance of being recognized.

The coracle was built at once. A light keel of laminated
and glued withe was shaped around pegs driven into
the float; ribs were bent and lashed into place; diagonal
ribs were attached to these, then the whole was covered
with four layers of varnished pad-skin.

At mid-morning of the fourth day after Barquan Blasdel's flight, the coracle, almost a canoe, departed to the
west, riding easily and swiftly over the sunny water. In
its gear was included the horn taken from Barquan
Blasdel's old workroom on Apprise Float. For three hours
it slid along the line of floats, each an islet bedecked in
blue, green, purple, orange, and black verdure, surmounted by the arching fronds of the prime plant, each
surrounded by its family of smaller pads. The coracle
reached the final float of the group and struck out to the
west, water swirling and sparkling behind the long oars.
Afternoon waned; the rain clouds formed and swept
across the sky, with black brooms hanging below. After
the rain came sunset, making a glorious display among
the broken clouds. The breeze began to blow; the sails
were raised; the men pulled in their oars and rested.
The coracle thrust swiftly west, with a chuckling of bow-
wave and wake. Then came the mauve dusk with the
constellations appearing, and then night with the stars
blazing down on the glossy black water. The men took
turns sleeping, and the night passed. Before dawn the
adverse wind rose; the men, saving their strength, rowed
only with enough force to maintain headway.

The second day passed in a like manner. The first line
of floats met by the flotilla fell behind, somewhat to the
north. Another day went by. The floats of the savages

failed to appear; presumably they had been passed in the night. Just before dawn of the fourth day the men lowered the horn into the water and listened.

Silence.

The men stood erect, looked into the west. Allowing for the increased speed of their passage, Tranque Float should be near at hand. But only a blank horizon could be seen.

At noon the men, increasingly dubious, ceased paddling and once more searched the horizon. As before, there was nothing visible save the line dividing dark blue from bright blue. The floats by now should be well within sight. Had they veered too far north or too far south?

The men deliberated and decided that while their own course had generally been true west, the original direction of flight might have been something south of east. In validation of this view was the fact that they had passed the intervening line of floats to the south. Hence the Old Floats in all probability lay behind the northern horizon. They agreed to paddle four hours to the north, then, if nothing was seen, to return to the south.

Toward the waning of afternoon, with the rain clouds piling up, far smudges showed themselves. Now they halted, lowered the horn, to hear *crunch crunch crunch* with startling loudness. The men twisted the tube to detect the direction of the sound. It issued from the north. Crouching low, they listened, ready to paddle hastily away if the sound grew louder. But it seemed to lessen, and the direction veered to the east. Presently it died to near-inaudibility, and the men proceeded.

The floats took on substance, extending both east and west; soon the characteristic profiles could be discerned, and then the hoodwink towers. Dead ahead was Aumerge, with Apprise Float yet to the west.

So they paddled up the chain, the floats with familiar and beloved names drifting past, floats where their ancestors had lived and died: Aumerge, Quincunx, Fay, Hastings, Quatrefoil, with its curious cloverleaf shape, and then the little outer group, The Bandings, and beyond, after a gap of a mile, Apprise Float.

The sun set, the hoodwink towers began to flicker, but the configurations could not be read. The men paddled the coracle toward Apprise. Verdure bulked up into the sky; the sounds and odors of the Old Floats wafted across the water, inflicting nostalgic pangs upon each of the men. They landed in a secluded little cove which had been described to them by Phyral Berwick, and covered the coracle with leaves and rubbish. According to the plan, two remained by the coracle, while the third, one Henry Bastaff, went off across the float toward the central common and Apprise Market.

Hundreds of people were abroad on this pleasant evening, but Henry Bastaff thought their mood to be weary and even a trifle grim. He went to the ancient Apprise Inn, which claimed to be the oldest building of the floats: a long shed beamed with twisted old stalks, reputedly cut at the astounding depth of three hundred feet. Within was a long buffet constructed of laminated strips, golden-brown with wax and use. Shelves to the rear displayed jars and tubes of arrack, beer, and spirits of life, together with various delicacies and sweetmeats. At the front wide eaves thatched with garwort frond shaded several dozen tables and benches where travelers rested and lovers kept rendezvous. Henry Bastaff seated himself where he could watch both the Apprise hoodwink tower and that of Quatrefoil to the east. The serving maid approached; he ordered beer and nut wafers. As he drank and ate, he listened to conversations at nearby tables and read the messages which flickered up and down the line of floats.

The conversations were uninformative; the hoodwink messages were the usual compendium of announcements, messages, banter. Then suddenly in mid-message came a blaze, all eighteen lights together, to signal news of great importance. Henry Bastaff sat up straight on the bench.

"Important . . . information! . . . This . . . afternoon . . . several . . . of . . . the . . . intercessors . . . kidnapped . . . by . . . the . . . rebels . . . returned . . . to . . . the . . . Floats . . . They . . . are . . . Barquan Blasdel . . . of

*. . . Apprise . . . with . . . his . . . spouse . . . and . . .
several . . . dependants . . . Vidal Reach . . . of . . . Sumber
. . . Luke Robinet . . . of . . . Parnassus . . . They . . .
have . . . a . . . harrowing . . . tale . . . to . . . tell . . .
The . . . rebels . . . are . . . established . . . on . . . a
. . . float . . . to . . . the . . . east . . . where . . . they
. . . kill . . . kragen . . . with . . . merciless . . . glee . . .
and . . . plan . . . a . . . war . . . of . . . extermination . . .
upon . . . the . . . folk . . . of . . . the . . . Old . . . Floats
. . . The . . . intercessors . . . escaped . . . and . . . after
. . . an . . . unnerving . . . voyage . . . across . . . the . . .
uncharted . . . ocean . . . late . . . today . . . landed . . . on
. . . Green Lamp Float . . . Barquan Blasdel . . . has . . .
called . . . for . . . an . . . immediate . . . convocation . . .
to . . . consider . . . what . . . measures . . . to . . . take
. . . against . . . the . . . rebels . . . who . . . daily . . . wax
. . . in . . . arrogance."*

Chapter 14

Six days later Henry Bastaff reported to the council of New Home Float. "Our arrival was precarious, for our initial direction took us many miles to the south of the Old Floats. Next time we must keep to the north of the floats intervening, whereupon we should make an easy landfall. Apparently the Blasdel coracle experienced even worse difficulties, for they reached Green Lamp Float about the same time we landed on Apprise. Possibly they delayed on one of our floats until they felt that we had given up pursuit. I sat at the Old Tavern when the news came, and I saw great excitement. The people seemed more curious than vindictive, even somewhat wistful. I heard no talk of King Kragen except one remark, somewhat ambiguous, to the effect that the rebels were perfectly welcome to attempt the slaughter of certain local kragen. A convocation was called for the following day. Since the folk of Almack Float would attend, I thought it best that Maible and Barway remain hidden. I stained my face swindler color, shaved away most of my eyebrows, pulled my hair forward, and wore a swindler's hood. I seemed the most inept of swindlers: half goon, half advertiser. At the convocation I looked eye to eye with my uncle Fodor the withe-peeler, who never turned for a second glance.

"The convocation was vehement and lengthy. Barquan Blasdel resumed his rank of Apprise Intercessor, without a moment's hesitation or as much as a by-your-leave. In my opinion Vrink Smathe, who had succeeded to the post, found no joy in Blasdel's return. He sat three rows back, bereft of his gown and nosepiece, frowning and blinking every time Blasdel spoke, which was almost continually.

"With great earnestness Blasdel called for a punitive expedition. He spoke of those who had departed as 'iconoclasts,' 'monsters,' 'vicious scum of the world,' which it was the duty of all decent folk to expunge.

"A certain number were stimulated, mostly those whom I would call the lowest element: folk of low prestige, unskilled, unknowledgeable and jealous of their betters. But these were few. In general he aroused only lukewarm attention. No one of importance showed heart for the project. The new intercessors in particular were less than enthusiastic. Clearly they covet their new posts, which they would lose if the old intercessors returned.

"Blasdel, seeing that he had aroused no vast sympathy for his wrongs, almost lost his temper, which is a rare thing to see in Barquan Blasdel. He accused those who were reluctant of cowardice and complacence, and so aroused antagonism. Everyone knows the temper of Emacho Feroxibus, Elder of the Quatrefoil Bezzlers. He is highly orthodox; still he is no poltroon. Very brusquely he instructed Blasdel to speak with a less pointed tongue. 'No one questions your zeal, but let it be applied to constructive purposes! What avail is there in destroying these folk? They are gone; good riddance. We shall maintain our ancient ways with more dedication because the dissidents have departed! I, for one, do not care to hear any further rabble-rousing!'

"I must say that Barquan Blasdel was not at all cowed. He said, 'It is all very well to temporize, and no one enjoys attempting an arduous and uncomfortable task such as the one I propose. Nevertheless these are unregenerates, creatures of the most depraved sort.'

"Feroxibus laughed in his face. 'If they are this evil, how did they allow you to live? Why did they not drown you?'

"Barquan Blasdel was taken aback. But he said, 'It is

clear enough. They feared discovery by King Kragen and planned that if the worst occurred, we would intercede in their behalf.'

"Emacho Feroxibus said no more, nor did Barquan Blasdel, and the convocation ended without any decisive acts.

"But this was only the convocation—the overt situation. I doubt if Barquan Blasdel was surprised by the lack of response. His last act was to call a meeting of all intercessors at the cottage of Vrink Smathe that evening.

"I went back to the coracle and conferred with Barway and Maible. Barway is a deep-diver. With this attribute in mind, and recalling the typical arrangement of an intercessor's workroom, we evolved a means to secure more information. Barway can tell you what occurred better than I."

Barway now made his report. He was a year or two younger than Henry Bastaff, an expert oarsman and a deep-diver of great endurance. He was an Advertiserman by caste, but had taken as a spouse the daughter of an Incendiary, and was generally held in high esteem. He spoke modestly, in a subdued manner.

"We made our plans while the sun was still high. I took a bearing on Smathe's hut, put on my goggles, ducked under the float. I don't know how many of you have swum under a float, but it's a beautiful sight. The water is deep blue, overhead is the white subskin and down below go the stems until finally they disappear into the depths.

"Smathe's hut was about seventy-five yards from the edge. This is a distance I can swim easily. But there and back, no. I would run out of air and drown under the float, unless I could find a hole like the one we found in Blasdel's hut. I trailed a rope so that I could be hauled back and revived if I failed to find the hut.

"But there was no problem. Seventy-five yards from the edge of the float I saw the dark hole above and the horn. I rose and floated in the hole. The plug was off. I was able to breathe.

"No one was in the workroom. In an outer chamber I heard voices, which seemed to be those of Vrink Smathe and his spouse. They were jointly lamenting the return of Barquan Blasdel. In fact, Smathe's spouse was upbraiding him for submitting so tamely to Barquan Blasdel's resumption of his position, and speaking in language quite unbecoming a woman of the Bezzlers, as I believe her caste to be.

"I did not linger. I made my rope fast to the horn, so that after dark I could find my way back. Then I returned to the coracle.

"We waited until evening. Henry Bastaff went back to Apprise Inn and listened to the talk, but heard nothing of consequence. As soon as we observed intercessors entering Smathe's hut, I took to the water, and guiding myself by the rope, returned to the hole in the Smathes' workroom."

At this the members of the council all gave a small shudder, since the under-water by night was a region of superstitious dread, especially under the pad: the locale of children's horror tales.

Barway continued. "I was early. The intercessors continued to come in as I waited. Vrink Smathe came to listen at the horn, and I was forced to submerge. I had taken little air and began to feel strain. Smathe turned the horn about, and I was forced to draw back when it pointed toward me. It stopped—and I realized that Smathe could hear my heartbeats. I swam to the other side of the hole and looked up through the water. Smathe was listening with his ear down and eyes turned away. I surfaced, took air, and went below once more." Barway laughed. The councilors responded with wry grimaces. Barway was understating the drama of the moment, as all knew.

"Smathe left the horn. I surfaced. I heard him say, 'For a moment I heard a curious pounding sound: a *thump thump thump*. But it went away.' Someone suggested that the sound was probably due to someone jumping on the float, and Smathe agreed to this. And then Blasdel came into the room."

Barquan Blasdel looked around the circle of intercessors, all of whom wore ceremonial black gowns with float emblems. He spoke first to Vrink Smathe. "Guards are posted against eavesdroppers?"

"Four apprentices stand outside the hut, with lanterns. No one may approach."

"Good. What we discuss now is of the utmost gravity and must not be disclosed, by deed or action.

"First of all, the intercessors now present must be ratified in their posts. Vidal Reach, Luke Robinet, and I relinquish our posts as Intercessors for Sumber, Parnassus, and Apprise, and now become Central Authorities. I hereby accede to the urgent suggestions made by many of you and will become Supreme Presiding Intercessor for all the floats. Luke Robinet and Vidal Reach will become my Chief Manciples.

"Now, to our main business. In spite of the timidity and inertia of the population, we cannot allow the rebels to continue in a state of insubordination. The reasons for this are many. First, they dared to attack King Kragen and to attempt his death: a deed of horror. Secondly, they kidnapped fifteen intercessors, a most heinous act. Third, even now they kill kragen with ever greater facility and already are preparing an assault upon King Kragen. Fourthly, even if they chose to remain quietly on their new floats, they represent a challenge to King Kragen's rule and thus to our authority. Fifthly, they have subjected me, Vidal Reach, Luke Robinet, and all the rest to the most repugnant indignities, thus by extension attacking the whole institution of intercessorship: which is to say ourselves. We must destroy them. Before I proceed, do I have your unanimous approval and endorsement of the viewpoints I have just presented?"

Endorsement was somewhat cautious but unanimous.

"These, then, are my proposals. We will organize a militia, to be called 'The Defenders,' or 'King Kragen's Admonitors,' or 'The People's Protectors,' or something similar. The able-bodied men of the New Floats number less than a thousand. Probably not more than five hundred would be fit to fight.

"To secure absolute and overwhelming strength we

must recruit a force of at least a thousand active, strong, and zealous young men. We shall train them in the use of weapons and, more importantly, wash from their minds all compunction, pity, or qualms against violence, and likewise do so in ourselves. I realize we thus contradict our oldest and most cherished tradition, but it is in a worthy cause.

"When the force is trained and equipped, we will embark in a suitable fleet of coracles, go forth and subdue the rebels. The most vicious and recalcitrant we must deal with definitely and finally; the rest shall be brought back in shame to the main floats and reduced to a new and low caste. Thus shall the lesson be driven home! Thus shall the power and benevolence of King Kragen be asserted! Thus shall we maintain and augment our own prestige!"

Barway reported the exhortations of Barquan Blasdel in as careful detail as he was able, in addition to the discussion that followed. No one had offered serious opposition to Barquan Blasdel's plan; there had only been a questioning as to ways and means.

"Did they announce a time schedule?" asked Phyral Berwick.

"I gather that they will begin immediately."

"I would expect as much." Phyral Berwick heaved a deep sigh. "Thus fear and pain and brutality come to the floats. It seems as if even in spite of our heritage we are little better than the folk of the Outer Worlds."

Sklar Hast said, "We must contrive countermeasures. First, there is no further point in keeping the intercessors captive. Better if now we give them a coracle and send them home. In this way they will learn nothing of our plans."

"What are our plans?" Arrel Sincere asked bleakly.

Sklar Hast considered. "We have a number of alternatives. We could train a militia of our own and trust to our own skill and strength. Ultimately, after much bloodshed, I fear we would be defeated. We could pack our belongings and flee once again, to seek a new far set

of floats. This is not an appealing idea. We can try to kill
King Kragen—but they would still attack us. Or we can
defeat our enemies by a strategy which so far I am unable to define. . . . In the meantime we must continue a
close observation of the Home Floats."

Chapter 15

On the world which had no name, there were no seasons, no variations of climate except those to be found by traversing the latitudes. Along the equatorial doldrums, where floats of sea-plant grew in chains and clots, each day was like every other, and the passage of a year could be detected only by watching the night sky. Though the folk had small need for accurate temporal distinctions, each day was numbered and each year named for some significant event. A duration of twenty-two years was a "surge" and was also reckoned by number. Hence a given date might be known as the 349th day in the Year of Malvinon's Deep Dive during the Tenth Surge. Time reckoning was almost exclusively the province of the scriveners. To most of the folk life was as pellucid and effortless as the grassy blue sea at noon.

King Kragen's attack upon Tranque Float occurred toward the year's end, which thereupon became the Year of Tranque's Abasement, and it was generally assumed that the following year would be known as the Year of the Dissenters' Going.

As the days passed and the year approached its midpoint, Barquan Blasdel, instead of allowing the memory of his kidnapping to grow dim, revived it daily with never-flagging virulence. Each evening saw a memorandum from Barquan Blasdel flicker up and down the chain of floats: "Vigilance is necessary! The dissidents are led by men of evil energy! They flout the majesty of King Kragen; they despise the folk who maintain old traditions and most especially the intercessors. They must be punished and taught humility. Should they dare to attack us, which is not beyond the limits of their megalomaniac viciousness, they must be hurled into the sea. To this end—King Kragen's Exemplary Corps!"

At a conclave of notables he made a speech of great earnestness, depicting the goals of the rebels in the most serious light, in which he was supported by those intercessors who had been liberated and who had made their way back to the Home Floats.

"Do we wish to see their detestable philosophy transplanted here?" demanded Barquan Blasdel. "A thousand times no! King Kragen's Exemplary Corps will act as one man to destroy the invading rebels, or, if a policy of cauterization is decided upon, to wipe out the central node of sepsis!"

Emacho Feroxibus, Elder of the Quatrefoil Bezzlers, was not moved by Barquan Blasdel's vehemence. "Let them be," he growled. "I have had long association with many of these folk, who are persons of high caste and good character. They obviously do not plan to invade the Home Floats; such a thought is absurd, and so long as they do not molest us, why should we molest them? No one should risk drowning for so dismal a cause."

Barquan Blasdel, containing his temper, explained carefully. "The matter is more complex than this. Here is a group who have fled in order to avoid paying their just due to King Kragen. If they are allowed to prosper, to make profit of their defection, then other folk may be tempted to wonder, why do we not do likewise? If the sin of kragen-killing becomes vulgar recreation, where is reverence? Where is continuity? Where is obedience to High Authority?"

"This may be true," stated Providence Dringle, Chief Hoodwink for the Populous Equity Float. "Nonetheless in my opinion the cure is worse than the complaint. And to risk a heretical opinion, I must say the benefits we derive from High Authority no longer seem commensurate with the price we pay."

Blasdel swung about in shock, as did the other intercessors. "May I ask your meaning?" Blasdel inquired icily.

"I mean that King Kragen consumes from six to seven bushels of choice sponges daily. He maintains his rule in the water surrounding the floats, true, but what do we need fear from the lesser kragen? By your own testimony the dissidents have developed a method to kill the kragen with facility."

Blasdel said with frigid menace, "I cannot overlook the fact that your remarks are identical to the preposterous ravings of the dissidents, who so rightly shall be obliterated."

"Do not rely on my help," said Providence Dringle.

"Nor mine," said Emacho Feroxibus. "I must also make note of the fact that while heretofore each float maintained the establishment of one intercessor, now there are two, not even to mention this corps of uniformed ruffians you are training."

"It is a distressing sight," said Barquan Blasdel in a voice quietly sad, "to see a man once effective and orthodox decline so suddenly into verbose senility. Emacho Feroxibus, speak on! Be sure that we will listen to you with the respect your advanced age and long career of service deserve! Talk as you will!"

Emacho Feroxibus's face was purple with rage. "You mealymouthed scoundrel! I'd teach you senility with my bare hands, were it not for my detestation of violence!"

The conclave shortly thereafter was adjourned.

King Kragen's Exemplary Corps was one thousand strong. Their barracks and training area was Tranque Float, which never had been restored to habitation. They wore a smart uniform, consisting of a gown somewhat like the intercessor's formal robes, black in front and white in back, with an emblem representing King Kragen sewed on the chest. They wore helmets of laminated pad-skin and rug-fish leather well-varnished, with the varnished dorsal fin of the gray-fish for a crest. For weapons they carried pikes of fine straight withe tipped with a blade of the hardest stem-wood, and daggers of simi-

lar quality. They lacked bows and arrows only because
none of the materials found on the floats or in the sea offered the necessary resilience. A dart thrower, on the order
of an atlatl, was tested, but accuracy was so poor that
it was discarded.

The Exemplary Corps, though it included men of every
caste and guild, was mainly comprised of those whose
careers were not proceeding with celerity or who dis-
liked toil with unusual vehemence. The other folk of the
floats regarded the Exemplars with mixed emotions. They
imposed something of a strain upon the normal functioning
of the economy, for they ate a great deal and produced
none of their own food. Meanwhile King Kragen daily
seemed to wax in size and appetite. The need for such a
large corps—or any corps at all—was continually ques-
tioned. Few accepted the intercessors' contention that the
dissidents planned an attack on the Home Floats.

Nevertheless the corps made a brave, if somewhat sinister show, parading in platoons of twenty with lances
aslant over their shoulders, or rowing their new twelve-
man coracles at great speed across the ocean whenever
King Kragen was not about. For the intercessors, dubious
of King Kragen's attitude, had kept from him the knowledge of the Exemplary Corps—though no one considered
it likely that he would forbid the organization if he knew
its aims.

Barquan Blasdel was commandant of the corps and
wore a uniform even more striking than that of the Exemplars: a split black and white gown, tied at the ankles,
with buttons of polished bindle-bane, purple epaulettes
carved to represent kragen mandibles, a purple helmet
with a crest simulating King Kragen's maw, with palps
and mandibles outspread: a fearsome sight.

Daily the corps drilled: running, jumping, thrusting
lances into dummies, springing in and out of their boats.
Daily they heard Barquan Blasdel discourse upon the
infamy of the rebels and the vileness of their habits.
Daily the corps performed a ritual expressing homage
and devotion to King Kragen and absolute obedience to
those who interceded with him. Most of the float not-

ables in private expressed disapprobation of the corps, and Emacho Feroxibus began to prepare an official sanction against the corps. Immediately King Kragen appeared at Quatrefoil Float, where Emacho Feroxibus was waste-elder, and remained four days, eating with great appetite. The Quatrefoil arbors were barren of sponges, and finally the folk of the float in desperation prevailed upon Emacho Feroxibus to modify his stand. He vented a great curse upon Barquan Blasdel, another upon the Exemplars, and a final objurgation against King Kragen, to the awe of all. Then he turned, a feeble and embittered man, and walked slowly to his hut.

King Kragen departed Quatrefoil Float. Three days later the body of Emacho Feroxibus was found floating in the lagoon, an apparent suicide, though many refuted this notion and claimed that in his grief he must have wandered blindly into the water. A few hinted of circumstances even more grim, but made no public assertion of their beliefs, since, if they were right, the message was clear.

The day arrived when in Barquan Blasdel's opinion King Kragen's Exemplary Corps was ready to perform the duty for which it was intended. Across Tranque Float went the word: "A week from today!"

A week later the sun went down and Tranque Float was taut with expectation. Barquan Blasdel, resplendent in his uniform, addressed the massed corps by torchlight.

"Brave members of the invincible Exemplary Corps! The time has come! The detestable vermin who live across the water pose a threat we can no longer tolerate. Already along these beautiful floats of our own, voices are whispering an envious desire for the depraved east of the rebels! We must win them back to the right way, the orthodox way! By persuasion if possible, by force if necessary! All bodes well! King Kragen has graciously given us leave to trespass upon his ocean and now relaxes near Helicon. So now—load boats! Rack pikes! Embark all! We sail to the east!"

A great hoarse shout rose from the Exemplars. With

a will the coracles were loaded; with rehearsed agility the Exemplars sprang aboard, thrust away from Tranque Float. Oars dug the water; with another great guttural call the coracles surged toward the east.

Dawn came; the water reflected the color of silver ash, then ruffled to the morning breeze. Big plum-blue square-sails were hoisted. They bellied; oars were shipped. The Exemplars rested. Ninety boats sailed the morning ocean, long low boats painted black and purple, with a white-and-black kragen blazoned on each straining sail. In each boat crouched 12 men in black-and-white gowns and black helmets with the spined crest.

Directly into the dazzle of the rising sun they sailed, and the glare served to conceal the boats that waited for them. When the breeze died and the sun had lifted, these boats were only a quarter-mile to the east: ten boats of strange design. They were twice as long as the twelve-man coracles, and each carried about twenty men. They waited in a line across the course of the Exemplar boats. The center boat, propelled by 16 oars, advanced. In the bow stood Sklar Hast.

He hailed the leading boat of the Exemplars. "What boats are you, and where are you bound?"

Barquan Blasdel rose to his feet. "Sklar Hast! You dare bring your boats so close to the Home Floats?"

"We sailed forth to meet you."

"Then you have sailed your last. We are bound to the new floats, to visit justice upon you."

"Turn back," said Sklar Hast. "Take warning! If you come farther, you are all dead men!"

Barquan Blasdel made a gesture to the other boats. "Forward! Pikes to hand! Board, kill, capture!"

"Stand back!" roared Sklår Hast. "Take warning, fools! Do you think we are helpless? Go back to the Home Floats and save your lives!"

The Exemplar coracles sped forward. That one in which Barquan Blasdel stood moved over to the side, to where he could command the battle. With only a hundred feet be-tween, men in the waiting boats suddenly rose to their feet, holding bows fashioned from kragen-turret splines.

They aimed, discharged arrows with flaming globular tips. The arrows struck into the black coracles, broke to spread flaming oil.

In the first volley twenty of the black-and-purple boats were aflame. In the second volley, forty flared up. In the third volley sixty. The withe and varnished pad-skin burned like tinder; fear-crazed Exemplars leaped into the sea. The thirty boats yet whole backed water, turned aside. Barquan Blasdel's boat already was out of range.

Sklar Hast steeled his heart, signaled. Another volley of flaming arrows set another ten boats aflame, and with an almost miraculous swiftness the proud black fleet of King Kragen's Exemplary Corps was destroyed.

"Forward!" Sklar Hast ordered. "One more volley. We must make a total end to this business!"

Reluctantly—for further action now seemed sheer slaughter—the archers lobbed a final volley of fire-arrows, and now, whether because the range was great or because the archers had no more will to attack, only eight boats were struck.

The water seethed with swimming shapes. As the coracles burned and collapsed, cases of stores floated loose, and the Exemplars clung to these.

Sklar Hast gave an order; the boats from New Float backed away from the scene of the battle. Cautiously those coracles still afloat returned. Stores and weapons were thrown overboard to lighten ship; swimming Exemplars were taken aboard to the limits of capacity, and ropes were thrown out to those yet floating.

Sluggishly, towing the men still in the water, the overloaded coracles returned across the sea toward Tranque Float.

Of the ninety proud black-and-purple boats which had set forth, twenty still floated.

Of a thousand Exemplars, five hundred survived.

Sklar Hast listened to the underwater horn and could detect nothing to indicate the proximity of King Kragen. He gave an order to his oarsmen, and the New Float boats followed the wallowing Exemplar fleet back to Tranque. To complete Barquan Blasdel's utter humiliation, when the black boats were a hundred yards from Tranque, the New Float boats moved in close, discharged two final volleys of fire-arrows, to destroy all the Exemplar coracles. All, Barquan Blasdel included, were forced to swim the last hundred yards to Tranque Float.

The following day a convocation was called on Apprise Float. There were none of the usual rambling introductory remarks. Morse Swin, the Apprise Arbiter, Phyral Berwick's one-time assistant, a big blond slow-spoken man, went to the rostrum. "Yesterday occurred a great tragedy, a futile useless tragedy, and all our wisdom is needed to resolve the situation. One thing is certain: reproaches are futile. The folly of attempting to attack the New Float has been made utterly evident, and it is high time that these so-called Exemplars put aside their pretensions or ideals or vanities—whatever one wishes to call them; I have heard each word used, as well as others. In any event, it is time that these idle men doff their uniforms and return to work."

Barquan Blasdel jumped to his feet. "Do I hear aright?" he called in a voice glacially cold.

Morse Swin looked at him in surprise. "Intercessor, if you please, I am speaking from the rostrum. When I am finished, you may have your turn."

"But I will not permit you to spout arrant nonsense. I thought to hear an impassioned urge for all men to rededicate themselves to what now must be our single concentrated goal—the absolute destruction of the rebels!"

"Intercessor, if you will restrain yourself, I wish to continue my remarks. I definitely take a less vehement view of the situation. We have our problems to solve; let us leave the folk of New Float to theirs."

Barquan Blasdel would not be quelled. "And what if they attack us?"

"They have shown no disposition to do so. They defended themselves and defeated you. If they planned an attack, they would never have allowed you to return to Tranque Float with your survivors. You should give thanks for your life and adjust yourself to the realities of the situation. I for one will hear of no further such ventures. The Exemplars must be disbanded and return to earning their living. This is my feeling, and I ask the approval of the convocation. Who agrees?"

There was vigorous assent.

"Who disagrees?"

In response came a sound of much lesser volume but much greater emotion. It issued from the throats of the intercessors and from the Exemplars themselves, who, wearing their uniforms and helmets, stood in four carefully ordered groups.

Morse Swin nodded his big, heavy head. "The verdict of the convocation seems definite; still, anyone who wishes is entitled to speak."

Barquan Blasdel came to the rostrum. He put his hands on the rail, turned his dark brooding gaze over the convocation. "You people who assented to the view of Morse Swin did so after only the most superficial attention. Shortly I will ask you to vote again.

"I wish to make three points.

"First, the setback of yesterday was unimportant. We shall win. Of that there is no doubt. Do we not have King Kragen on our side? We withdrew after sustaining losses, it is true. Do you know why this was made necessary? Because upon these floats, perhaps here at the convocation, at this very moment, there are spies. Furtive, skulking creatures of the most perverted and amoral attitudes imaginable! We expected no serious opposition; we set sail—but the spies had sent word ahead! The rebels prepared a dastardly and cruel ambush. What fiends these rebels are, to hurl fire at defenseless boats! Our drowned comrades will not go unavenged, I assure you! Do I speak truth, comrade Exemplars?"

From the uniformed groups came an impassioned shout: "Truth!"

Barquan Blasdel looked slowly around the convocation. "Morse Swin spoke of realities. He is the man who is not realistic. King Kragen is benevolent, but he is now wrathful. His is the might, his is the force! We cannot deny

him! He has ordained that his Exemplars act, he has
given them sharp weapons fashioned from the hardest
stem, he has given them his endorsement! The Exemplars act in King Kragen's behalf. They are men of true
faith; they are forbearing and benevolent, as is King
Kragen, but like King Kragen, they are terrible in their
wrath. King Kragen's Exemplary Corps must not be
contravened! They know the path of rectitude, which is
derived from the will of King Kragen; they will not be
denied! When an Exemplar speaks, he speaks with the
voice and the will of King Kragen! Do not oppose or contradict or fail to obey! Because first to be feared are the
sharp weapons, the daggers and pikes, and second, the
source of all awe and majesty, King Kragen himself. I,
his Intercessor, and Chief Exemplar, assure you of the
'reality' of this situation. Who should know better?

"We now enter a time of emergency! All must look as
with a single gaze to the east, toward the float of the
rebels. All must harden their minds, put aside the soft
ways of ease, until the rebels are destroyed and the emergency is ended.

"During this emergency we require a strong authority,
a central coordinating mind to ensure that all proceeds
with efficiency. I have attempted to withdraw myself from
a post of such responsibility, but all insist that I take this
terrible burden upon myself. I can only, with humility,
profess my readiness to make this personal sacrifice, and
I now so proclaim this emergency and this assumption of
absolute authority. I will be pleased to hear a unanimous
and hearty endorsement."

From the Exemplars and the intercessors came a great
call. Elsewhere were frozen faces and indignant mutters.

"Thank you," said Barquan Blasdel. "The unanimity
of the endorsement will be duly noted in the records. The
convocation is now adjourned. When circumstances warrant, when the emergency is at an end, I will announce
the fact and call another convocation. All may now return to your home floats. Instructions as to how you best
may serve King Kragen will be forthcoming."

Sputtering with anger, Morse Swin jumped to his feet.

"One moment! Are you insane? This is not traditional procedure! You did not call for adverse voices!"

Barquan Blasdel made a small, quiet signal to a near-by group of Exemplars. Ten of these stalked forward, seized Morse Swin by the elbows, hustled him away. He struggled and kicked; one of the Exemplars struck him on the back of the head with the haft of his dagger.

Barquan Blasdel nodded placidly. "I did not call for adverse voices because there was obvious unanimity. The convocation is adjourned."

Chapter 16

Henry Bastaff described the convocation to a silent conclave of notables on New Home Float. "There was no core of opposition, no firmness. Old Emacho Feroxibus was dead, Morse Swin had been dragged off. The folk were stunned. The situation was too fantastic to be credible. No one knew whether to laugh or scream or tear the Exemplars apart with their bare hands. They did nothing. They dispersed and went back to their huts."

"And now Barquan Blasdel rules the floats," said Phyral Berwick.

"With the most exacting rigor."

"So then we must expect another attack."

Henry Bastaff agreed. "Without any doubt whatever."

"But how? Surely they won't attempt another raid!"

"As to this, I can't say. They might build boats with shields to divert fire-arrows, or evolve a system to throw fire-arrows of their own."

"Fire-arrows we can tolerate," said Sklar Hast. "We can build our boats with kragen-hide rather than padskin; this is no great threat.... I can't imagine how Blasdel hopes to attack us. Yet undoubtedly he does so intend."

"We must continue our surveillance," said Phyral Berwick. "So much is evident." He looked at Henry Bastaff. "Are you willing to return?"

Bastaff hesitated. "The risk is great. Blasdel knows that we spy on him. The Exemplars will be very much on the alert...I suspect that the best information will be gained from under the pad, under the intercessor's hut. If Barway and Maible will return, I will accompany them."

Phyral Berwick clapped him on the shoulder. "You have the admiration and gratitude of us all! Because now our very lives depend upon information!"

Four days later Roger Kelso took Sklar Hast to Outcry Float, where he pointed out another contrivance whose function or purpose Sklar Hast could not fathom. "You will now see electricity produced," said Roger Kelso.

"What? In that device?" Sklar Hast inspected the clumsy apparatus. A tube of hollow stalk five inches in diameter, supported by a scaffold, rose twenty feet into the air. The base was held at one end of a long box containing what appeared to be wet ashes. The far end of the box was closed by a slab of compressed carbon, into which were threaded copper wires. At the opposite end, between the tube and the wet ashes, was another slab of compressed carbon.

"This is admittedly a crude device, unwieldy to operate and of no great efficiency," said Kelso. "It does, however, meet our peculiar requirements: which is to say, it produces electricity without metal, through the agency of water pressure. Brunet describes it in his Memorium. He calls it the 'Rous machine' and the process 'cataphoresis.' The tube is filled with water, which is thereby forced through the mud, which here is a mixture of ashes and sea-slime. The water carries an electric charge which it communicates to the porous carbon as it seeps through. By this means a small but steady and quite dependable source of electricity is at our hand. As you may have guessed, I have already tested the device and so can speak with confidence."

He turned, signaled his helpers. Two clamped shut the box of mud, others mounted the scaffold, carrying buckets of water which they poured into the tube. Kelso connected the wires to a coil of several dozen revolutions. He brought forward a dish. On a cork rested a small rod of iron.

"I have already 'magnetized' this iron," said Kelso. "Note how it points to the north? It is called a 'compass' and can be used as a navigational device. Now—I bring it near the end of the coil. See it jerk! Electricity is flowing in the wire!"

Sklar Hast was much impressed. Kelso spoke on. "The process is still in a crude state. I hope eventually to build pumps propelled by the wind to raise the water, or even a generator propelled by the wind, when we have much more metal than we have now. But even this Rous machine implies a dramatic possibility. With electricity we can disassociate sea-water to produce the acid of salt, and a caustic of countering properties as well. The acid can then be used to produce more highly concentrated streams of electricity—if we are able to secure more metal. So I ask myself, where do the savages procure their copper? Do they slaughter young kragen? I am so curious that I must know, and I plan to visit the Savage Floats to learn their secret."

"No," said Sklar Hast. "When they killed you, who would build another Rous machine? No, Roger Kelso. What was MacArthur's Dictum: 'No man is indispensable'? It is incorrect. You are too important to risk. Send your helpers, but do not venture yourself into danger. The times are too troubled for you to indulge yourself in the luxury of dying."

Kelso gave a grudging acquiescence. "If you really believe this."

Sklar Hast returned to New Home Float, where he sought out Meril Rohan. He enticed her aboard a small coracle and rowed east along the line of floats. Upon a little pad floating somewhat to the south of the line, they halted and went ashore and sat under a thicket of wild sugar-stem. "Here," said Meril, "is where we can build our home, and this is where we shall have our children."

Sklar Hast sighed. "It is so peaceful, so calm, so beautiful. . . . Think how things must be on the Home Floats, where that madman rules!"

"If only all could be peaceful. . . . Perhaps chaos is in our nature, in the nature of man!"

"It would seem," said Sklar Hast, chewing on a stalk of sugar-stem, "that we of the floats should by all rationality be less prone to these qualities. The Firsts fled the Outer Worlds because they were subjected to oppression; hence it would seem that their mildness and placidity, after twelve generations, would be augmented in us."

Meril gave a mischievous laugh. "Let me tell you my theory regarding the Firsts." She did, and Sklar Hast was first amused, then incredulous, finally indignant. "What a thing to say! These are the Firsts! Our ancestors! You are an iconoclast in all truth! Is this what you teach the children? In any event, it is all so ridiculous!"

"I don't think so. So many things are explained. So many curious passages become clear, so many ambiguous musings and what would seem irrational regrets are clarified."

"I refuse to believe this! Why—it's . . ." Words deserted him. Then he said, "I look at you, and I watch your face, and I think you are a product of the Firsts, and I know what you say is impossible."

Meril Rohan laughed in great merriment. "But just think, if it's so, then perhaps the Outer Worlds would not be such dreadful places as we have previously believed."

Sklar Hast shrugged. "We'll never be sure—because we can never leave this world."

"Do you know what someday we'll do? Not you or I, but perhaps our children or their children. They'll find the Ship of Space, they'll dive or send down grapples and raise it to the surface. Then they'll study it very carefully. Perhaps there'll be much to learn, perhaps nothing. . . . But just think! Suppose they could contrive a way to fly space once more, or at the very least to send out some sort of message!"

"Anything is possible," said Sklar Hast. "If your violently unorthodox theory is correct, if the Firsts were as you seem to believe, then this might be a desirable goal." He sighed once more. "You and I will never see it; we'll never know the truth of your theories—which perhaps is just as well."

A coracle manned by Carl Snyder and Roble Baxter, two of Roger Kelso's helpers, sailed west to the Savage Floats. Nine days later they returned, gaunt, sunburned but triumphant. Carl Snyder reported to the counsel of elders: "We waited offshore until dark. The savages sat around a fire, and using a telescope, we could see them clearly. They are a wretched folk: dirty, naked, ugly. When they were asleep, we approached and found a spot where we could hide the coracle and ourselves. Three days we watched the savages. There are only twenty or thirty. They do little more than eat, sleep, copulate, and smelt copper. First they heat the husks of their sponges to a char. This char they pulverize and put into a pot to which a bellows is attached. As they work the bellows, the charcoal glows in many colors, and finally dissipates, and the copper remains."

"And to think that for twelve generations we have thrown sponge husks into the sea!" cried Kelso in anguish.

"It would seem," reflected Sklar Hast, "that the kragen derive the copper of their blood from sponges. Where, then, is the source of iron in our own blood? It must be found in some article of our own diet. If the source was found, we would not need to drain ourselves pale to obtain pellets."

"We test every substance we can lay our hands on," said Kelso. "We have created a white powder and a yellow powder, but no metal. Naturally we continue with our tests."

Several days later Kelso once more invited Sklar Hast to Outcry Float. Under four long open-sided sheds 50 men and women worked at retorts fashioned from ash cemented with sea-ooze. Bellows puffed, charcoal glowed, fumes billowed up and drifted away through the foliage.

Kelso showed Sklar Hast a container of copper pellets. Sklar Hast reverently trickled the cold, clinking shapes through his fingers. "Metal! All from kragen blood?"

"From kragen blood and organs, and from the husks of sponges. And here—here is our iron!" He showed Sklar Hast a container holding a much smaller quantity of iron

—a handful. "This represents a hundred bleedings. But we have found iron elsewhere: in glands of the gray-fish, in the leaves of bindlebane, in purple-weed pith. Small quantities, true, but before we had none."

Sklar Hast hefted the iron. "In my imagination I see a great engine constructed of iron. It floats on the water and moves faster than any coracle. King Kragen sees it. He is awed, he is taken aback, but in his arrogance he attacks. The engine thrusts forth an iron knife; iron hooks grip King Kragen, and the iron knife hacks him in two." Once again Sklar Hast let the pellets of iron sift through his fingers. He shook his head ruefully. "We might bleed every man, woman, and child dry a hundred times, a thousand times, and still lack iron to build such a kragen-killing engine."

"Unfortunately true," said Roger Kelso. "The engine you suggest is out of our reach. Still, using our wits, perhaps we can contrive something almost as deadly."

"We had better make haste. Because Barquan Blasdel and his Exemplars think only of bringing some terrible fate to us."

Whatever the fate Barquan Blasdel planned for the folk of New Home Float, he kept his own counsel. Perhaps he had not yet perfected the plan; perhaps he wished to consolidate the authority of the Exemplars; perhaps he suspected that spies gauged his every move. In this latter conjecture he was accurate. Henry Bastaff, in the role of an itinerant spice-grinder, frequented Apprise Inn with ears angled toward the Exemplars who customarily relaxed from their duties here.

He learned little. The Exemplars spoke in large voices, hinting of portentous events, but it was clear that they knew nothing.

Occasionally Barquan Blasdel himself would appear, wearing garments of new and elaborate style. Over a tight black coverall he wore a jacket, or surplice, of embroidered purple strips, looped around shoulders, chest, waist, and thighs. From his shoulders extended a pair of extravagantly wide epaulettes, from which hung a black cloak, which flapped and billowed as he walked. His headdress was even more impressive: an elaborate bonnet of pad-skin cusps and prongs, varnished and painted black and purple—a symbolic representation of King Kragen's countenance.

Barquan Blasdel's dark, gaunt face was sober and harsh these days, though his voice, when he spoke, was as easy and relaxed as ever, and generally he managed a slight smile, together with an earnest forward inclination of the head, which gave the person to whom he spoke a sense of participation in affairs of profound importance.

Barway and Maible had taken elaborate precautions against the vigilance of the Exemplars. Their coracle was submerged and tucked under the edge of the float; working from underwater, they had cut rectangular niches up into the pulp of the float, with a bench above water-level and ventilation holes up through the top surface into the shadow of a hessian bush. In these niches they lay during daylight hours, making occasional underwater visits to the hole in Vrink Smathe's workroom. By night they came forth to eat the food brought by Henry Bastaff.

Like Henry Bastaff, they had learned nothing. Barquan Blasdel and the Exemplars seemed to be marking time. King Kragen made his usual leisurely circuit of the floats. Twice Henry Bastaff saw him and on each occasion marveled at his size and might. On the evening after the second occasion, sitting at his usual place to the back of Apprise Inn, he heard a brief snatch of conversation which he considered significant. Later in the evening he reported to Barway and Maible.

"This may mean something or nothing; it is hard to judge. I personally feel that something is afoot. In any event these are the circumstances. A pair of blackguards had come in from Sumber, and a Felon Elder asked regarding Thrasneck and Bickle. The blackguards replied that all the previous month they had worked at Thrasneck Lagoon, building sponge-arbors in profusion: enough to serve not only Thrasneck, but Tranque, Bickle, Sumber, Adelvine, and Green Lamp as well. These arbors were of a new design, heavier and more durable, and buoyed by bundles of withe rather than bladders. The Felon Elder then spoke of sponge barges his guild brothers were building on Tranque: a project supposedly secret, but why maintain secrecy about a set of sponge barges? It wasn't as if they were attack boats for the Exemplars. Here a group of Exemplars came into the inn and the conversation halted."

"Sponge arbors and barges," mused Maible. "Nothing immediately sinister here."

"Not unless the intent is to provision a new expeditionary force."

"Something is in the wind," said Henry Bastaff. "Intercessors both new and old are arriving at Apprise, and there's talk of a conclave. You two keep your ears on Smathe's workroom, and I'll try to catch a word or two of what's happening."

Mid-morning of the following day Henry Bastaff walked by the hessian bush under which lay Barway and Maible. Squatting, pretending to tie the thongs of his sandals, he muttered: "Bastaff here. Today is the conclave, highly important, beside the hoodwink tower. I'm going to try to hide behind a stack of hood-facings. I may or may not be successful. One of you swim to where the tower posts go through the float. There's a gap of a few inches where you can breathe and possibly hear—especially if you chisel away some of the pulp."

From under the fronds of the hessian bush came a muffled voice. "Best that you keep your distance; they'll be on the alert for spies. We'll try to hear the proceedings from below."

"I'll do whatever looks safe," said Henry Bastaff. "I'm going. There's an Exemplar watching me."

In their niche below the pad, Maible and Barway heard his retreating footsteps and, a moment later, another leisurely tread, as someone, presumably the Exemplar, strolled by.

The footsteps moved away; Barway and Maible relaxed.

After consultation, Barway slipped from the shelf into

the water, and after taking his bearings, swam to where the poles of the hoodwink tower passed through the float. Here, as Bastaff had stated, were gaps at which, after a certain amount of cutting and chiseling, Barway could either put his mouth and nose or his ear, but not both at once.

Henry Bastaff went about his business of spice-grinding, and after an hour or so walked past the hoodwink tower. The pile of hood-facings was as before. Henry Bastaff looked in all directions. No one appeared to be observing him. He squatted, shifted the facings this way and that and contrived an opening into which he inserted himself.

Time passed. The longer Henry Bastaff sat the more uneasy he became. The pile of facings suddenly seemed overprovident. The area had been too conveniently deserted. Could it be that the facings had been arranged to serve as a spy-trap?

Hurriedly Bastaff wriggled back out, and after a quick look around, took himself off.

A half hour later intercessors began to gather on the scene. Six Exemplar Selects came to stand guard, and to prevent unauthorized persons from pressing too close.

At last Barquan Blasdel appeared, walking slowly, his black cloak drifting and billowing behind. Three Exemplars of the Fervent category marched at his back. He passed near the stack of facings and turned them a quick glance. They had been disarranged, slightly moved. Barquan Blasdel's lips tightened in a small, secret smile. He turned, spoke to the Fervent Exemplars, who took up positions beside the pile of facings.

Barquan Blasdel faced the assembled intercessors. He raised his hands for silence.

"Today begins a new phase of our preparations," he said. "We expect to achieve two purposes: to systematize our relations with King Kragen, and to establish a necessary precondition to our great project. Before I go into details, I wish to make some comments in regard to espionage. No creature is as vile as a spy, especially a spy from the dissident floats. If apprehended, he can expect but small mercy at our hands. So now I inquire: have all present been vigilant in this regard?"

The assembled intercessors nodded their heads and gave witness that, indeed, they had exercised meticulous caution.

"Good!" declared Barquan Blasdel heartily. "Still, the dissident spies are clever and viciously militant. They know no more fear than a spurgeon, and even less guilt for their misdeeds. But we are more clever than these spies. We know how to smell them out! In fact, the rank odor of an unmitigated spy issues from behind that stack of hood-facings. Fervents! Take the necessary measures!"

The Exemplar Fervents tore into the stack of hood-facings. Barquan Blasdel came to watch. The Fervents found nothing. They looked at Barquan Blasdel, who pulled at his lip in annoyance. "Well, well," said Blasdel. "A vigilance too extreme is preferable to carelessness."

Below, where the pole passed through the float, Barway, by dint of taking a deep breath and holding his ear to the crevice, had heard the last remark. But now Barquan Blasdel returned to his previous place, and his words became muffled and incomprehensible.

Barquan Blasdel spoke for several minutes. All listened attentively, including the six Exemplars Barquan Blasdel had put on guard, to such an extent that presently they stood at the last row of the intercessors. Barquan Blasdel finally noticed and waved them back. One of these, more punctilious than the others, retreated past the edge of the hoodwink supply shed, where a man stood listening. "Ho!" called the Exemplar. "What do you do here?"

The man so detected gave a wave of all-indulgent tolerance and staggered drunkenly away.

"Halt!" cried the Exemplar. "Return and declare yourself!" He jumped forward and dragged the man forth into the open area. All examined him with attention. His skin was dark, his face was bland and bare of hair; he wore the nondescript snuff-colored smock of a Peculator or Malpractor.

Barquan Blasdel marched forward. "Who are you? Why do you lurk in these forbidden precincts?"

The man staggered again and made a foolish gesture. "Is this the tavern? Pour out the arrack, pour for all! I am a stranger on Apprise—I would know the quality of your food and drink."

Vrink Smathe snorted. "The fool is a spice-grinder and drunk. I have seen him often. Direct him to the inn."

"No!" roared Blasdel, jerking foward in excitement. "This is a dissident, this is a spy! I know him well! He has shaved his head and his face, but never can he defeat my acuity! He is here to learn our secrets!"

The group turned their attention upon the man, who blinked even more vehemently. "A spy? Not I. I seek only a cup of arrack."

Blasdel sniffed the air in front of the captive's face. "There is no odor: neither beer nor arrack nor spirits of life. Come! All must satisfy themselves as to this so that there will be no subsequent contradictions and vacillations."

"What is your name?" demanded Vogel Womack, the Adelvine Intercessor. "Your float and your caste? Identify yourself!"

The captive took a deep breath, cast off his pretense of drunkenness. "I am Henry Bastaff. I am a dissident. I am here to find if you plan evil against us. That is my sole purpose."

"A spy!" cried Barquan Blasdel in a voice of horror. "A self-confessed spy."

The intercessors set up a chorus of indignant hoots. Blasdel said: "He is guilty of at least a double offense: first, the various illegalities entering into his dissidence; and second, his insolent attempt to conspire against us, the staunch, the faithful, the true! As Chief Exemplar, I am compelled to demand the extreme penalty."

Vogel Womack tried to temper Barquan Blasdel's wrath. "Let us delay our judgment," he remarked uneasily. "Presently the man's deed may not appear so grave."

Barquan Blasdel ignored him. "This man is a vile dissident, an agent of turmoil and a spy. He must suffer an extreme penalty! To this declaration there will be allowed no appeal!"

Henry Bastaff was taken to Vrink Smathe's dwelling, which stood nearby, and confined in the workroom, with four Exemplars surrounding him and never for an instant taking away their gaze.

Henry Bastaff surveyed the surroundings. To right and left were shelves; at the back a screen concealed the hole through the float.

Henry Bastaff spoke to the Exemplars. "I heard Blasdel's program. Are you men interested in what is to happen?"

None responded.

Henry Bastaff smiled wanly and looked toward the quarter of the room in which was the hole. "Blasdel intends to lead King Kragen to the new floats, so that King Kragen may express his pleasure against the dissidents, and may also destroy whatever dissident boats stand in the way."

No one spoke.

"To this end," said Henry Bastaff in a clear and distinct voice, "he has built floating sponge arbors to guarantee King Kragen an ample ration during the voyage, together with barges for more sponges, boats for the necessary advertisermen and a force of Exemplars to occupy New Home Float."

The four men in uniform merely stared at him. After a few minutes Henry Bastaff repeated the information. He added: "I may never see the New Floats again, but I hope I h 've helped us to freedom. Farewell to the men of the New I ats; I wish only that they could be warned of the evil which Barquan Blasdel plans to bring to them."

"Silence!" spoke one of the Exemplars. "You have ranted enough."

Chapter 17

On the following day an alteration was made in the method by which King Kragen was tendered his oblation. Previously, when King Kragen approached a lagoon with the intent of feasting, arbors overgrown with sponges were floated to the edge of the net, for King Kragen to pluck with his palps. Now the sponges were plucked by advertisermen, heaped upon a great tray and floated forth between a pair of coracles. When the tray was in place, Barquan Blasdel went to Vrink Smathe's workroom, where he seemed not to see Henry Bastaff. He listened at the horn. King Kragen was close at hand; the scraping of his chitin armor sounded loud in the earpiece. Blasdel turned the crank which sent forth the summoning rattle. King Kragen's scraping ceased, then began once more, increasing in intensity. King Kragen was approaching.

He appeared from the east, turret and massive torso riding above the surface, the great rectangular platform gliding through the ocean on easy strokes of his vanes.

The forward eyes noted the offering. He eased forward, inspected the tray, and with his forward palps began to scoop the sponges into his maw.

From the float folk watched in somber speculation. Barquan Blasdel came forth to stand on the edge of the pad, to bow and gesticulate ritual approval as King Kragen ate.

The tray was empty. King Kragen made no move to

181

depart. Blasdel swung about, called to a Fervent Exemplar. "The sponges—how many were offered?"

"Seven bushels. King Kragen usually eats no more."

"Today he seems to hunger. Are others plucked?"

"Those for the market, another five bushels."

"They had best be tendered King Kragen; it is not well to stint."

While King Kragen floated motionless, the coracles were pulled to the float. Another five bushels were poured upon the tray and the tray thrust back toward King Kragen. Again he ate, consuming all but a bushel or two. Then, replete, he submerged till only his turret remained above water. And there he remained, moving sluggishly a few feet forward, a few feet backward.

Nine days later Maible and Barway, haggard as much from horror as privation, reported to the folk of New Float. "On the following day King Kragen had not yet moved. It was clear that the new method of feeding had impressed him favorably. So at noon the tray was again filled, with at least ten bushels of sponge, and again King Kragen devoured the lot.

"During this time Henry Bastaff was moved from Smathe's workroom, and we could not learn of his new place of incarceration. This saddened us, for we had intended to attempt his rescue through the horn hole.

"On the third day Blasdel made an announcement which went across the hoodwink towers, to the effect that King Kragen had demanded the privilege of executing the dissident spy who had sinned so grievously against him. At noon the tray went out. At the very top was a wide board supporting a single great sponge, and below, the usual heap. King Kragen had not moved fifty yards for three days. He approached the tray, reached for the topmost sponge. It seemed fastened to the board. King Kragen jerked, and so decapitated Henry Bastaff, whose head had been stuffed into the sponge. It was a horrible sight, with the blood spouting upon the pile of sponges. King Kragen seemed to devour them with particular relish.

"With Henry Bastaff dead, we no longer had reason to delay—except for curiosity. King Kragen showed no signs of moving, of visiting other floats. It was clear that he found the new feeding system to his liking. On the fourth day his meal was furnished by Granolt Float and ferried to Apprise by coracle. On the fifth day the sponges were brought from Sankston. It appears that King Kragen is now a permanent guest at Apprise Float—which is the essential first part of Blasdel's plan."

There was a moment or two of silence. Phyral Berwick made a sound of revulsion. "It is a situation which we must alter." He looked at Sklar Hast. "How far advanced are your preparations?"

Sklar Hast indicated Roger Kelso. "Ask the man who smelts our metal."

"Our resources are multiplying," said Kelso. "We have bled everyone on the float, twice or three times; this blood has yielded ten pounds of iron, which we have hammered and refined. It is now hard and tough beyond all belief—but still there is only ten pounds. The kragen and the sponge husks have given us much more copper: fifty or sixty pounds at a guess. Our electrical device has produced twenty-four flasks of acid of salt, which we maintain in bottles blown in our glass shop. This is now an establishment completely separated from the smelting."

"Encouraging and interesting," said Robin Magram, the Master Incendiary, a man not too imaginative, "but how will it avail against King Kragen?"

"We haven't completed our experiments," said Kelso. "I can't give you a definite answer—yet. We need a live kragen, and they've been giving us a wide berth. Perhaps we'll be forced to go hunting."

"Meanwhile," said Sklar Hast, "we can disrupt Blasdel's timetable."

A month later, in the dead of night, with only starlight to guide them, six black coracles approached Tranque Float. It showed a barren unfamiliar silhouette, denuded of all verdure save for the central spikes and their attendant fronds. At the eastern end of the float were low barracks and a flat area apparently used as an exercise ground; at the western end was a bleak construction area, where the skeletons of sponge arbors glimmered white in the starlight.

The net across the lagoon mouth was cut. The coracles drifted into the lagoon, where were ranked long arbor after arbor, each bulging with ripe sponges. The men made silent play with knives, cutting away the withe floats and the anchor ropes; the arbors submerged, disappeared; the water of the lagoon rippled blank and vacant.

The coracles departed as stealthily as they had come. They circled the float. From the eastern side of Tranque, toward Thrasneck Float, extended six floating fingers to which were moored twelve double-hulled barges. Oil was poured into each hull, torches were flung; great flames thrust high into the sky, and angry cries came from the barracks. The black boats, with the men in black straining to the paddles, fled eastward across the ocean. For an hour the orange flames licked at the sky, then slowly dwindled and died.

Two months later, a scout coracle, after a cautious reconnaissance, returned to report that the docks had been repaired, that new barges were nearly complete, that new arbors were in place, and that the area was patrolled continuously by Exemplars armed with pikes and swords.

Chapter 18

The year, which subsequently became known as the Year of the Exemplars, came to an end. Shortly after the beginning of the new year, three swindlers, working the water to the east of Tranque Float, sighted a fleet approaching from the east. The two younger swindlers made a hurried motion to haul in their lines, but the elder halted them. "Our business is swindling, no more. Let the boats go by; they will not molest us."

So the swindlers sat back and watched the flotilla pass. There were twelve galleys, rather high of freeboard, sheathed with a dull black membrane. Each carried a crew of thirty who sat low and rowed through holes in the hull, and thus were protected from missiles. They wore casques and corselets of the same black membrane that sheathed the hulls, and beside each was a bow, a dozen arrows with fire-bulb tips, a long lance with a tang of orange metal. The galleys accompanied a strange rectangular barge riding on three hulls. Platforms fore and aft supported a pair of bulky objects concealed by tarpaulins, with beside each a tub. In each of the three hulls were rows of squat glass vats, two hundred and ten in all, each of two quarts capacity, each two-thirds full of pale liquid. Like the galleys, the barge was propelled by oarsmen sitting low in the hulls and protected from hostile missiles by the screen of black membrane.

The Exemplars on Tranque Float observed the flotilla, and hoodwink towers flickered an alarm: "*The... dissi-*

*dents . . . are . . . returning . . . in . . . force . . . They . . .
come . . . in . . . strange . . . black . . . canoes . . . and . . .
an . . . even . . . more . . . peculiar . . . black . . . barge . . .
They . . . show . . . no . . . fear."*

Returning came instruction in a code unintelligible to those of the flotilla. They could now see the Tranque docks where the new barges floated and where already the laden armors had been brought forth to be attached and towed astern. The docks swarmed with Exemplars, ready to defeat any attempt to destroy the barges a second time. But the flotilla sailed past, and the hoodwink towers flickered once again: *"The . . . dissidents . . . proceed . . . west . . . They . . . are . . . passing . . . Tranque Float . . . It . . . is . . . difficult . . . to . . . conjecture . . . their . . . intent."* And back came coded instructions, evidently advising cautious observation, for the Exemplars boarded coracles and rowed on a course parallel to the flotilla, keeping a cautious two hundred yards between.

The flotilla continued up the line of floats: Thrasneck, Bickle, Green Lamp; at last Fay, Quatrefoil, and finally Apprise.

In the water before the lagoon lolled King Kragen— a bloated monstrous King Kragen, dwarfing the entire flotilla.

King Kragen became aware of the boats. He swung about, the monstrous vanes sucking whirlpools into the ocean. The eyes with opalescent films shifting back and forth fixed upon the black sheathing of galleys, armor, and barge, and he seemed to recognize the substance of kragen hide, for he emitted a snort of terrible displeasure. He jerked his vanes, and the ocean sucked and swirled.

The barge swung sidewise to King Kragen. The tarpaulins were jerked away from the platforms at either end, to reveal massive crossbow-like mechanisms fashioned from laminated stalk and kragen chitin, with cables woven from strips of kragen-leather. Two teams of men turned a windlass hauling back the great cross-arms. Into the channels were placed iron harpoons smelted from human blood. In the holds other men lowered four thousand plates of iron and copper into the glass vats.

King Kragen sensed menace. Why else should men be so bold? He twitched his vanes, inched forward—to within a hundred feet. Then he lunged. Vanes dug the water; with an ear-shattering shriek King Kragen charged, mandibles snapping.

The men at the crossbows were pale as sea-foam; their fingers twitched. Sklar Hast turned to call: "Fire!" but his voice caught in his throat and what he intended for an incisive command came forth as a startled stammer. The command was nevertheless understood. The left crossbow thudded, snapped; the harpoon, trailing a black cable, sprang at King Kragen's turret, buried itself. King Kragen hissed.

The right crossbow thudded, snapped; the second harpoon stabbed deep into the turret. Sklar Hast motioned to the men in the hold. "Connect!" The men joined copper to copper. In the hold two hundred and ten voltaic cells, each holding ten thin-leaved cathodes and ten thin-leaved anodes, connected first in series of seventy, and these series in parallel, poured a gush of electricity along the copper cables wrapped in varnished pad-skin leading to the harpoons. Into and through King Kragen's turret poured the energy, and King Kragen went stiff. His vanes protruded at right angles to his body. Sklar Hast laughed—an explosion of nervous relief. "King Kragen is amenable, no less than the smaller kragen."

"I never doubted," said Roger Kelso.

They dove into the water, along with 20 others. They swam to King Kragen, clambered up the rigid subsurface platform; with mallets and copper chisels they attacked the lining between dome and turret wall.

On Apprise Float a great throng had gathered. One man, running back and forth, was Barquan Blasdel. He leaped into one of the coracles and, screaming orders, led the Exemplars against the dissident flotilla. Fire-arrows cut arcs across the sky; seven coracles burst into flames, and the Exemplars plunged into the water. The others swerved aside. Barquan Blasdel issued the most strenuous commands, but the Exemplars made no new sorties.

King Kragen floated stiff and still—eyes staring, palps protruding. His turret was thirty feet in circumference, but twenty-two men hacked with chisels, and now the lining was broken. Bars were inserted into the crack, all heaved. With a splitting sound the dome was dislodged. It slid over and in falling pulled away one of the harpoons. The circuit was broken; King Kragen once more owned his self-control.

For one galvanic instant he lay quiescent, trembling. Then he gave vent to an appalling scream, a sound which sent the folk on the float to their knees.

King Kragen hurled himself out of the water. The men who had hacked away his turret were flung far and wide, all except three who had managed to reach into the turret and cling to the knotted gray cords. One of these was Sklar Hast. While King Kragen lunged and thrashed, he slashed at the nerve nodes with his iron knife. Again King Kragen screamed, and thrust himself into the ocean. Water crashed down into the turret; two men were washed away. Sklar Hast, with arms and legs clenched among the strands, alone remained in place. The salt water on the exposed brain caused King Kragen great discomfort, and he sprang back out of the water, bent double. Sklar Hast hewed and hacked; the vanes, palps, and mandibles jerked, contracted, twisted, snapped in accordance. King Kragen's vehemence lessened; he floated moaning with vanes dangling limp. Some of the men who had been flung away swam back; in a ceremony both dreadful and exalted King Kragen's nerve nodes were torn out and cast into the sea.

King Kragen floated limp, a lifeless hulk. The men plunged into the sea to wash themselves, swam back to the barge. The flotilla now eased toward Apprise Float. Sklar Hast stood on the forward platform. Barquan Blasdel cried to the folk: "To arms! Stakes, chisels, mallets, knives, bludgeons! Smite the miscreants!"

Sklar Hast called to the throng: "King Kragen is dead. What do you say to this?"

There was silence; then a faint cheer, and a louder cheer, and finally uproarious celebration.

Sklar Hast pointed a finger at Barquan Blasdel. "That man must die. He organized the Exemplars. He murdered Henry Bastaff. He has fed your food to the vile King Kragen. He would have continued doing so until King Kragen overgrew the entire float."

Barquan Blasdel cried to his Exemplars: "Weapons at ready! Any who attack—kill!"

Sklar Hast called to the Exemplars: "Throw down your weapons! You are finished. King Kragen is dead. You are Exemplars only to a dead sea-beast."

Barquan Blasdel looked quickly in all directions. His Exemplars, outnumbered by the men of the float, showed no disposition to fight. Barquan Blasdel laughed brassily and turned away. "Hold!" called Morse Swin, the Apprise Arbiter. "Barquan Blasdel, return! You must face the verdict of a convocation!"

"Never! Not I!" Barquan Blasdel tried to push through the throng, and this was a mistake, for it triggered the counter-impulse to halt him. When he was touched, he smote, and again he erred, for the blow brought a counter-blow and Barquan Blasdel was presently torn to pieces. The crowd now turned upon the Exemplars, and all those who were unable to escape to the coracles shared Barquan Blasdel's fate. Those who fled in the coracles were intercepted by the black galleys, herded into a clot, where they surrendered themselves.

"Come ashore, men of the New Floats; deliver us the Exemplars, that they may be served like their fellows!" cried one from the float.

Another voice called, "Come greet your old friends, who long have been saddened at your absence!"

And another voice cried, "Tonight the arrack will flow; come drink your share! Tonight the yellow lamps will burn; we will play the pipes and dance; come dance in the light of our yellow lamps!"

Sklar Hast considered a moment, then he replied, "We will come ashore, and we will deliver the prisoners. Let us have no more frantic bloodshed, however. Those who have committed crimes, let them face a convocation and be punished or freed according to our ancient traditions. Is it agreed? Otherwise we must return to New Floats!"

Morse Swin called out, "We agree in all respects! Enough blood has been spilled; we want no more!"

"Then we come ashore, to rejoice with you!"

And the black boats of the New Floats landed upon Apprise; the men went ashore to greet old friends, caste-fellows and guild-brothers.

The corpse of King Kragen floated in the ocean, a desolate hulk. Already dusk had come; the hoodwink towers flickered in all earnest; from Tranque in the east to Almack and Sciona in the far west flashed the news. Intercessors stared mournfully across the water. Exemplars divested themselves of their uniforms and sheepishly mingled with those whom so recently they had treated with arrogance. They were derided and vilified, but none were injured; the mood of the folk was too rich and full. Before every hut yellow lamps flared; the oldest arrack, the most mellow spirits of life were brought forth; old friends drank together. All night, under the white constellations. there was revelry and joy and great thanksgiving that never again need the folk of the floats serve King Kragen or another like him.